don't erase me

don't erase me

S T O R I E S

Carolyn Ferrell

Houghton Mifflin Company

BOSTON   NEW YORK

For information about permission to reproduce selections from
this book, write to Permissions, Houghton Mifflin Company,
215 Park Avenue South, New York, New York 10003.

For information about this and other Houghton Mifflin trade and reference
books and multimedia products, visit The Bookstore at Houghton Mifflin on
the World Wide Web at http://www.hmco.com/trade/.

"Proper Library" first appeared in *Ploughshares* and was reprinted in *The Best
American Short Stories 1994* and in *Children of the Night: Best Short Stories
by Black Writers, 1967 to the Present* (Boston: Little, Brown, 1995); "Don't
Erase Me" first appeared in *Story;* "Can You Say My Name?" in *Streetlights:
Illuminating Tales of the Urban Black Experience,* edited by Doris Jean Austin
(New York: Penguin, 1996); "Tiger-Frame Glasses" in *Ploughshares;* "Wonder-
ful Teen" in *Literary Review;* "Miracle Answer" in *Fiction;* and "Inside, a
Fountain" in *Girls* (Atlanta: Global City, 1997).

Library of Congress Cataloging-in-Publication Data

Ferrell, Carolyn.
Don't erase me : stories / Carolyn Ferrell.
p.   cm.
ISBN 0-395-71327-7
I. Title.
PS3556.E72572D66   1997
813'.54—dc21   96-29646   CIP

Book design by Anne Chalmers
Type: New Caledonia (Adobe)

Printed in the United States of America

QUM 10 9 8 7 6 5 4 3 2

For my mother,

ELKE SCHMIDT FERRELL BLUTH

"That is the trouble with the whole lot of unno. All unno think bout is judgement and future life. But from morning me study seh in this country fe yu God is a one eye God. Him only open him good eye to people who have everything already so him can pile up more things on top of that. Him no business with rag tag and bobtail like unno. God up a top a laugh keh keh keh at the likes of you. Fe see you, so poor and turn down think you can talk to the likes of him so high and mighty. Keh keh keh."

"Jacko!"

"Fe yu God ever help anybody yu know?"

"Plenty time."

> — Olive Senior,
> "Country of the One Eye God"

Silent friend of many distances, feel
how your breath enlarges all of space.

And if the earthly no longer knows your name,
whisper to the silent earth: I'm flowing.
To the flashing water say: I am.

> — Rainer Maria Rilke,
> *Sonnets to Orpheus*, II, 29

contents

don't erase me

proper library

BOYS, MEN, GIRLS, children, mothers, babies. You got to feed them. You always got to keep them fed. Winter summer. They always have to feel satisfied. Winter summer. But then you stop and ask, Where is the food going to come from? Because it's never-ending, never-stopping. Where? Because your life is spent on feeding them and you never stop thinking about where the food is going to come from.

Formula, pancakes, syrup, milk, roast turkey with corn-bread stuffing, Popsicles, love, candy, tongue kisses, hugs, kisses behind backs, hands on faces, warmth, tenderness, Boston cream pie, fucking in the butt. You got to feed them, and it's always going to be you. Winter summer.

My ma says to me, Let's practice the words this afternoon when you get home, baby. I nod to her. I don't have to use any words with her to let her know I will do what she wants. When family people come over and they see me and Ma in the kitchen like that with the words, they say she has the same face as the maid in the movies. She does have big brown hands like careful shovels, and she loves to touch and pat and warm you up with them. And when she walks, she shuffles. But if anyone is like the maid in the movies, it is Aunt Estine. She likes to give mouth, specially when I got the kids on my hands. She's sassy. She's got what people call a bad attitude. She makes sure you hear her heels clicking all the time, specially when you are lying in bed before dawn and thinking things in order, how you got to keep moving, all day long. Click, click. Ain't nobody up yet? Click. Lazy ass Negroes you better not be specting me to cook y'all breakfast when you do get up! Click, click. I'm hungry. Click. I don't care what time it is, I'm hungry y'all and I'm tired and depressed and I need someone to talk to. Well the hell with all y'all. That's my last word. Click, click, click.

My ma pats her hands on my schoolbag, which is red like a girl's, but that's all right. She pats it like it was my head. The books I have in it are: Biology, Woodworking for You, Math 1, The History of Civilization.

I'm supposed to be in Math 4, but the people keep holding me back. I know it's no real fault of mine. I been teaching the kids Math 4 from a book I took out of the Lending Mobile in the schoolyard. The kids can do most of Math 4. They like the way I teach it to them, with real live explanations, not the kind where you are supposed to have everything already in your head and it's just waiting to come out. And the kids don't ask to see if I get every one right. They trust me. They trust my smart. They just like the feel of the numbers and seeing them on a piece of paper: division of decimals, division of fractions. It's these numbers that keep them moving and that will keep them moving when I am gone. At school I just keep failing the City-Wide Tests every May and the people don't ask any questions: they just hold me back. Cousin Cee Cee said, If you wasn't so stupid you would realize the fact of them holding you back till you is normal.

The kids are almost as sad as Ma when I get ready to go to school in the morning. They cry and whine and carry on and ask me if they can sit on my lap just one more time before I go, but Ma is determined. She checks the outside of my books to make sure nothing is spilled over them or that none of the kids have torn out any pages. Things got to be in place. There has to be order if you gonna keep on moving, and Ma knows that deep down. This morning I promise to braid Lasheema's hair right quick before I go, and as I'm braiding, she's steady smiling her four-year-old grin at Shawn, who is a boy and therefore has short hair, almost a clean shave, and who can't be braided and who weeps with every strand I grease, spread, and plait.

Ma warns me, Don't let them boys bother you now, Lorrie. Don't let 'em.

I tell her, Ma, I have not let you down in a long time. I know what I got to do for you.

She smiles but I know it is a fake smile, and she says, Lorrie, you are my only son, the only real man I got. I don't want them boys to get you from me.

I tell her because it's the only thing I can tell her, You cooking up something special tonight?

Ma smiles and goes back to fixing pancake mix from her chair in the kitchen. The kids are on their way to forgetting about me 'cause they love pancakes more than anything and that is the only way I'll get out of here today. Sheniqua already has the bottle of Sugar Shack syrup and Tonya is holding her plate above her nappy lint head.

Tommy, Lula Jean's navy husband, meets me at the front door as I open it. Normally he cheers me up by testing me on Math 4 and telling me what a hidden genius I am, a still river running deep, he called it one time. He likes to tell me jokes and read stories from the Bible out loud. And he normally kisses my sister Lula Jean right where I and everybody else can see them, like in the kitchen or in the bedroom on the bed, surrounded by at least nine kids and me, all flaming brown heads and eyes. He always says, This is what love should be. And he searches into Lula Jean's face for whole minutes.

I'm leaving for Jane Addams High School and I meet Tommy and he has a lady tucked under his arm and it ain't Lula Jean. Her hair is wet and smells like mouthwash and I hate him in a flash. I never hate anybody, but now I hate him. I know that when I close the door behind me, a wave of mouths will knock Tommy and this new lady down, but it won't drown them. My sister Anita walks into the room and notices and carries them off into the bathroom, quick and silent. But before that she kisses me on my cheek and pats her hand, a small one of Ma's, on my chest. She whispers, You are my best man, remember that. She slips a letter knife in my jacket pocket. She says, If that boy puts his thing on you, cut it off. I love you, baby. She pushes me out the door.

Layla Jackson who lives in the downtown projects and who might have AIDS comes running up to me as I walk out our building's door to the bus stop. She is out of breath. I look at her and could imagine a boy watching her chest heave up and down like that and suddenly getting romantic feelings, it being so big and all, split like two kickballs bouncing. I turn my eyes to hers, which are crying. Layla Jackson's eyes are red. She has her baby Tee Tee in her arms, but it's cold out here and she doesn't have a blanket on him or nothing. I say to her, Layla, honey, you gonna freeze that baby to death.

And I take my jacket off and put it over him, the tiny miracle.

Layla Jackson says, Thanks Lorrie man I got a favor to ask you please don't tell me no please man.

Layla always makes her words into a worry sandwich.

She says, Man, I need me a new baby sitter 'cause I been took Tee Tee over to my mother's but now she don't want him with the others and now I can't do nothing till I get me a sitter.

I tell her, Layla, I'm going back to school now. I can't watch Tee Tee in the morning but if you leave him with me in the cafeteria after fifth period I'll take him on home with me.

She says, That means I got to take this brat to Introduction to Humanities with me. Shit, man. He's gonna cry and I won't pass the test on Spanish Discoverers. Shit, man.

Then Layla Jackson thinks a minute and says, Okay, Lorrie, I'll give Tee to you at lunch in the cafeteria, bet. And I'll be 'round your place 'round six for him or maybe seven, thanks, man.

Then she bends down and kisses Tee Tee on his forehead and he glows with what I know is drinking up an oasis when you are in the desert for so long. And she turns and walks to the downtown subway, waving at me. At the corner she comes running back because she still has my jacket and Tee Tee is waving the letter knife around like a flag. She says that her cousin Rakeem was looking for me and to let me know he would be waiting for me 'round his way. *Yes.* I say to her, See you, Layla, honey.

Before I used to not go to Jane Addams when I was supposed to. I got in the habit of looking for Rakeem, Layla's cousin, underneath the Bruckner Expressway, where the Spanish women sometimes go to buy oranges and watermelons and apples cheap. He was what you would call a magnet, only I didn't know that then. I didn't understand the different flavors of the pie. I saw him one day and I had a feeling like I wanted him to sit on my lap and cradle me. That's when I had to leave school. Rakeem, he didn't stop me. His voice was just as loud as the trucks heading toward Manhattan on the Bruckner above us: This is where your real world begins, man. The women didn't watch us. We stared each other in the eyes. Rakeem taught me how to be afraid of school and of people watching us. He said, Don't go back, and I didn't. A part of me was saying that his ear was more delicious than Math 4. I didn't go to Jane Addams for six months.

On the BX 17 bus I see Tammy Ferguson and her two little ones and Joe Smalls and that white girl Laura. She is the only white girl in these Bronx projects that I know of. I feel sorry for her. She has blue eyes and red hair, and one time when the B-Crew-Girls were going to beat her butt in front of the building, she broke down crying and told them that her real parents were black from the South. She told them she was really a Negro and they all laughed and that story worked the opposite than we all thought. Laura became their friend, like the B-Crew-Girls' mascot. And now she's still their friend. People may laugh when she ain't around but she's got her back covered. She's loyal and is trying to wear her thin flippy hair in cornrows, which in the old days woulda made the B-Crew, both boys and girls, simply fall out. When Laura's around, the B-Crew-Girls love to laugh. She looks in my direction when I get on the bus and says, Faggot.

She says it loud enough for all the grown-up passengers to hear. They don't look at me, they keep their eyes on whatever their eyes are on, but I know their ears are on me. Tammy Ferguson always swears she would never help a white girl, but now she can't pass up this opportunity, so she says, You tight-ass homo, go suck some faggot dick. Tammy's kids are taking turns making handprints on the bus window.

I keep moving. It's the way I learned: keep moving. I go and sit next to Joe Smalls in the back of the bus and he shows me the Math 3 homework he got his baby's mother Tareen to do for him. He claims she is smarter now than when she was in school at Jane Addams in the spring. He laughs.

The bus keeps moving. I keep moving even though I am

sitting still. I feel all of the ears on us, on me and Joe and the story of Tareen staying up till 4 A.M. on the multiplication of fractions and then remembering that she had promised Joe some ass earlier but seeing that he was sound asleep snoring anyway, she worked on ahead and got to the percent problems by the time the alarm went off. Ha ha, Joe laughs, I got my girl in deep check. Ha ha.

All ears are on us, but mainly on me. Tammy Ferguson is busy slapping the babies to keep quiet and sit still, but I can feel Laura's eyes like they are a silent machine gun. Faggot faggot suck dick faggot. Now repeat that one hundred times in one minute and that's how I am feeling.

Keep moving. The bus keeps rolling and you always have to keep moving. Like water like air like outer space. I always pick something for my mind. Like today I am remembering the kids and how they will be waiting for me after fifth period and I remember the feel of Lasheema's soft dark hair.

Soft like the dark hair that covers me, not an afro but silky hair, covering me all over. Because I am so cold. Because I am so alone. A mat of thick delicious hair that blankets me in warmth. And therefore safety. And peace. And solitude. And ecstasy. Lasheema and me are ecstatic when we look at ourselves in the mirror. She's only four and I am fourteen. We hold each other, smiling.

Keep moving. Then I am already around the corner from school while the bus pulls away with Laura still on it because she has fallen asleep in her seat and nobody has bothered to touch her.

On the corner of Prospect Avenue and Westchester where the bus lets me out, I see Rakeem waiting for me. I am not supposed to really know he's there for me and he is not supposed to show it. He is opening a Pixie Stick candy and then he fixes his droopy pants so that they are hanging off the edge of his butt. I can see Christian Dior undies. When I come nearer he throws the Pixie Stick on the ground next to the other garbage and gives me his hand just like any B-Crew-Boy would do when he saw his other crew member. Only we are not B-Crew members, we get run over by the B-Crew.

He says, Yo, man, did you find Layla?

I nod and listen to what he is really saying.

Rakeem says, Do you know that I got into Math 3? Did you hear that shit? Ain't that some good shit?

He smiles and hits me on the back and he lets his hand stay there.

I say, See what I told you before, Rakeem? You really got it in you to move on. You doing all right, man.

He grunts and looks at his sneakers. Last year the B-Crew-Boys tried to steal them from him but Rakeem screamed at them that he had AIDS from his cousin and they ran away rubbing their hands on the sides of the buildings on the Grand Concourse.

Rakeem says, Man, I don't have nothing in me except my brain that tells me: Nigger, first thing get your ass up in school. Make them know you can do it.

I say, Rakeem, you are smart, man! I wish I had your smart. I would be going places if I did.

He says, And then, Lorrie, I got to get people to like me and to stop seeing me. I just want them to think they like me. So I got to hide *me* for a while. Then you watch, Lorrie, man: *much* people will be on my side!

I say to him, Rakeem, you got Layla and baby Tee Tee and all the teachers on your side. And you got smart. You have it made.

He answers me after he fixes his droopy pants again so that they are hanging exactly off the middle of his ass: Man, they

8

are wack! You know what I would like to do right now, Lorrie? You know what I would like? Shit, I ain't seen you since you went back to school and since I went back. Hell, you know what I would like? But it ain't happening 'cause you think I'ma look at my cousin Layla and her bastard and love them and that will be enough. But it will never be enough.

I think about sitting on his lap. I did it before but then I let months go by because it was under the Bruckner Expressway and I believed it could only last a few minutes. It was not like the kind of love when I had the kids because I believed they would last forever.

He walks backwards away, and when he gets to the corner he starts running. No one else is on the street. He shouts, Rocky's Pizza! I'ma be behind there, man. We got the school fooled. This is the master plan. I'ma be there, Lorrie! *Be there.*

I want to tell Rakeem that I have missed him and that I will not be there but he is gone. The kids are enough. The words are important. They are all enough.

The front of Jane Addams is gray-green with windows with gates over all of them. I am on the outside.

The bell rings first period and I am smiling at Mr. D'Angelo and feeling like this won't be a complete waste of a day. The sun has hit the windows of Jane Addams and there is even heat around our books. Mr. D'Angelo notices me but looks away. Brandy Bailey, who doesn't miss a thing, announces so that only us three will hear, Sometimes when a man's been married long he needs to experience a new kind of loving, ain't that what you think, Lorrie?

For that she gets thrown out of the classroom and an extra

day of in-school suspension. All ears are now on me and Mr. D'Angelo. I am beyond feeling but I know he isn't. And that makes me happy in a way, like today ain't going to be a complete waste of a day.

He wipes his forehead with an imported handkerchief. He starts out saying, Class, what do we remember about the piston, the stem, and the insects? He gets into his questions and his perspiration stops and in two minutes he is free of me.

And I'm thinking: Why couldn't anything ever happen, why does every day start out one way hopeful but then point to the fact that ain't nothing ever going to happen? The people here at school call me ugly, for one. I know I got bug eyes and I know I am not someone who lovely things ever happen to, but I ask you: Doesn't the heart count? Love is a pie and I am lucky enough to have almost every flavor in mine. Mr. D'Angelo turns away from my desk and announces a surprise quiz and everybody groans and it is a sea of general unhappiness but no one is more than me, knowing that nothing will ever happen the way I'd like it to, not this flavor of the pie. And I am thinking, Mr. D'Angelo, do you know that I would give anything to be like you, what with all your smarts and words and you know how to make the people here laugh and they love you. And I would give anything if you would ask me to sit on your lap and ask me to bite into your ear so that it tingles like the bell that rips me in and out of your class. I would give anything. Love is a pie. Didn't you know that? Mr. D'Angelo, I am in silent love in a loud body.

So don't turn away. *Sweat.*

Mrs. Cabrini pulls me aside and whispers, My dear Lorrie, when are you ever going to pass this City-Wide? You certainly have the brains. And I know that your intelligence will take you far, will open new worlds for you. Put your mind to your dreams, my dear boy, and you will achieve them. You are your own universe, you are your own shooting star.

People 'round my way know me as Lorrie and the name stays. Cousin Cee Cee says the name fits and she smacks her gum in my face whenever she mentions that. She also adds that if anyone ever wants to kick my ass, she'll just stand around and watch because a male with my name and who likes it just deserves to be watched when whipped.

Ma named me for someone else. My real name is Lawrence Lincoln Jefferson Adams. It's the name on my school records. It's the name Ma says I got to put on my application to college when the time comes. She knows I been failing these City-Wide Tests and that's why she wants to practice words with me every day. She laughs when I get them wrong but she's afraid I won't learn them on my own, so she asks me to practice them with her and I do. Not every day, but a whole lot: look them up and pronounce them. Last Tuesday: *Independence. Chagrin. Symbolism. Nomenclature. Filament.* On Wednesday, only: *Apocrypha.* Ma says they have to be proper words with proper meanings from a dictionary. You got to say them right. This is important if you want to reach your destiny, Ma says.

Like for instance the word *Library.* All my life I been saying that "Liberry." And even though I knew it was a place to read and do your studying, I still couldn't call it right. Do you see what I mean? I'm about doing things, you see, *finally* doing things right.

Cousin Cee Cee always says, What you learning all that shit for? Don't you know it takes more than looking up words to get into a college, even a damn community college? Practicing words like that! Is you a complete asshole?

And her two kids, Byron and Elizabeth, come into the kitchen and ask me to teach them the words too, but Cee Cee says it will hurt their eyes to be doing all that reading and besides they are only eight and nine. When she is not around I give them words with up to ten letters, then they go back to TV with the other kids.

When we have a good word sitting, me and Ma, she smoothes my face with her hands and calls me Lawrence, My Fine Boy. She says, You are on your way to good things. You just got to do things the proper way.

We kiss each other. Her hands are like the maid in the movies. I know I am taken care of.

Zenzile Jones passes me a note in History of Civilization. It's the part where Ptolemy lets everyone know the world is round. Before I open it, I look at her four desks away and I remember the night when I went out for baby diapers and cereal and found her crying in front of a fire hydrant. I let her cry on my shoulder. I told her that her father was a sick man for sucking on her like that.

The note says, Please give me a chance.

Estine Smith, my mother's sister who wants me and the kids to call her by both names, can't get out of her past. Sometimes I try on her clothes when I'm with the kids and we're playing dress-up. My favorite dress is her blue organza without the back. I seen Estine Smith wear this during the daytime and I fell in love with it. I also admired her for wearing a dress with the back out in the day, but it was only a ten-second admiration. Because then she opens her mouth and she is forever in her past. Her favorite time to make us all go back to is when they lynched her husband, David Saul Smith, from a tree in 1986 and called the TV station to come and get a look. She can't let us go one day without reminding us in words. I never want to be like her, ever. Everybody cries when they are in her words because they feel sorry for her, and Estine Smith is not someone but a walking hainted house.

Third period. I start dreaming about the kids while the others are standing in line to use the power saw. I love to dream about the kids. They are the only others who think I am beautiful besides Ma and Anita. They are my favorite flavor of the pie, even if I got others in my mind.

Most of the time there are nine but when my other aunt, Samantha, comes over I got three more. Samantha cries in the kitchen and shows Ma her blue marks and it seems like her crying will go on forever. Me, I want to take the kids' minds away. We go into Ma's room where there is the TV and we sing songs like "Old Gray Mare" and "Bingo Was His Name O" or new ones like "Why You Treat Me So Bad?" and "I Try to Let Go." Or else I teach them Math 4. Or else I turn on the TV so they can watch Bugs or He-Man and so I can get their ironing done.

Mc, I love me some kids. I need me some kids.

Joe Smalls talks to me in what I know is a friendly way. The others in Woodworking for You don't know that. They are like the rest of the people who see me and hear the action and latch on.

Joe Smalls says, Lorrie, man, that bitch Tareen got half the percentage problems wrong. Shit. Be glad you don't have to deal with no dumb-ass Tareen bitch. She nearly got my ass a F in Math 3.

I get a sad look on my face, understanding, but it's a fake look because I'm feeling the rest of the ears on us, latching, readying. I pause to heaven. I am thinking I wish Ma had taught me how to pray. But she doesn't believe in God.

Junior Sims says, Why you talking that shit, Joe, man? Lorrie don't ever worry about bitches!

Perry Samson says, No, Lorrie never ever thinks about pussy as a matter of fact. Never ever.

Franklin says, Hey, Lorrie, man, tell me what you think about, then? What can be better than figuring out how you going to get that hole, man? Tell me what?

Mr. Samuels, the teacher, turns off the power saw just when it gets to Barney Moore's turn. He has heard the laughter from underneath the saw's screeching. Everybody gets quiet. His face is like a piece of lumber. Mr. Samuels is never soft. He doesn't fail me even though I don't do any cutting or measuring or shellacking. He wants me the hell out of there.

And after the saw is turned off, Mr. Samuels, for the first time in the world, starts laughing. The absolute first time. And everybody joins in because they are afraid of this and I laugh too because I'm hoping all the ears will go off me.

Mr. Samuels is laughing Haw Haw like he's from the country. Haw Haw. Haw Haw. His face is red. Everyone cools down and is just smiling now.

Then he says, Class, don't mess with the only *girl* we got in here!

Now it's laughter again.

Daniel Fibbs says, Yeah, Mr. Samuels is *on!*

Franklin laughs, No fags allowed, you better take your sissy ass out of here 'less you want me to cut it into four pieces.

Joe Smalls is quiet and looking out the window.

Junior Sims laughs, Come back when you start fucking bitches!

Keep moving, keep moving.

I pick up my red bag and wade toward the door. My instinct is the only thing that's working, and it is leading me back to Biology. But first out the room. Inside me there is really nothing except for Ma's voice: *Don't let them boys.* But inside there is nothing else. My bones and my brain and my heart would just crumble if it wasn't for that swirling wind of nothing in me that keeps me moving and moving.

Perry laughs, I didn't know Mr. Samuels was from the South.

With his eyelashes, Rakeem swept the edges of my face. He let me know they were beautiful to him. His face went in a circle around mine and dipped in my eyes and dipped in my mouth. He traveled me to a quiet place where his hands were the oars and I drifted off to sleep. The thin bars of the shopping cart where I was sitting in made grooves in my back, but it was like they were rows of tender fingers inviting me to stay. The roar of the trucks was a lullaby.

Layla Jackson comes running up to me but it's only fourth period because she wants to try and talk some sense into Tyrone. She hands me little Tee Tee. Tyrone makes like he wants to come over and touch the baby but instead he flattens his back against the wall to listen to Layla. I watch as she oozes him. In a minute they are tongue kissing. Because they are the only two people who will kiss each other. Everyone says that they gave themselves AIDS and now have to kiss each other because there ain't no one else. People walk past them and don't even notice that he has his hand up her shirt, squeezing the kickball.

Tee Tee likes to be in my arms. I like for him to be there.

The ladies were always buying all kinds of fruits and vegetables for their families underneath the Bruckner Expressway. They all talked Spanish and made the sign of the cross and asked God for forgiveness and gossiped.

Rakeem hickeyed my neck. We were underneath the concrete bridge supports and I had my hands on the handle of a broken shopping cart, where I was sitting. Don't go back,

Rakeem was telling me, don't go back. And he whispered in my ear. And I thought of all the words I had been practicing, and how I was planning to pass that City-Wide. Don't go back, he sang, and he sat me on his lap and he moved me around there. They don't need *you*, he said, and *you* don't need *them*.

But I do, I told him.

This feeling can last forever, he said.

No, it can't, I said, but I wound up leaving school for six months anyway. That shopping cart was my school.

I am thinking: It will never be more. I hold Tee Tee carefully because he is asleep on my shoulder and I go to catch the BX 17 back to my building.

Estine Smith stays in her past and that is where things are like nails. I want to tell her to always wear her blue organza without the back. If you can escape, why don't you all the time? You could dance and fling your arms and maybe even feel love from some direction. You would not perish. *You* could be free.

When I am around and she puts us in her past in her words, she tells me that if I hada twitched my ass down there like I do here, they woulda hung me up just by my black balls.

The last day Rakeem and I were together, I told him I wanted to go back, to school, to everyone. The words — I tried to explain about the words to Rakeem. I could welcome him into my world if he wanted me to. Hey, wasn't there enough room for him and me and the words?

Hell no, he shouted, and all the Spanish women turned around and stared at us. He shouted, You are an ugly-ass bastard who will always be hated big-time and I don't care what you do: this is where your world begins and this is where your world will end. Fuck you. You are a pussy, man. Get the hell out of my face.

Ma is waiting for me at the front door, wringing her hands. She says it's good that I am home because there is trouble with Tommy again and I need to watch him and the kids while she goes out to bring Lula Jean home from the movies, which is where she goes when she plans on leaving Tommy. They got four kids here and if Lula Jean leaves, I might have to drop out of school again because she doesn't want to be tied to anything that has Tommy's stamp on it.

I set Tee Tee down next to Tommy on the sofa bed where I usually sleep. Tommy wakes up and says, Hey, man, who you bringing to visit me?

I go into the kitchen to fix him some tea and get the kids' lunch ready. Sheniqua is playing the doctor and trying to fix up Shawn, who always has to have an operation when she is the doctor. They come into the kitchen to hug my legs and then they go back in the living room.

Tommy sips his tea and says, Who was that chick this morning, Lorrie, man?

I say I don't know. I begin to fold his clothes.

Tommy says, Man, you don't know these bitches out here nowadays. You want to show them love, a good time, and a real deep part of yourself and all they do is not appreciate it and try to make your life miserable.

He says, Well, at least I got Lula. Now that's some woman.

And he is asleep. Sheniqua and her brother Willis come in and ask me if I will teach them Math 4 tonight. Aunt Estine rolls into the bedroom and asks me why do I feel the need to take care of this bum, and then she hits her head on the doorframe. She is clicking her heels. She asks, Why do we women feel we always need to teach them? They ain't going to learn the right way. They ain't going to learn shit. That's why we always so alone. Click, click.

The words I will learn before Ma comes home are: *Soliloquy, Disenfranchise, Catechism.* I know she will be proud. This morning before I left she told me she would make me a turkey dinner with all the trimmings if I learned four new words tonight. I take out my dictionary but then the kids come in and want me to give them a bath and baby Tee Tee has a fever and is throwing up all over the place. I look at the words and suddenly I know I will know them without studying.

And I realize this in the bathroom and then again a few minutes later when Layla Jackson comes in cursing because she got a 60 on the Humanities quiz. She holds Tee but she doesn't touch him. She thinks Tyrone may be going to some group where he is meeting other sick girls and she doesn't want to be alone. She curses and cries, curses and cries. She asks me why things have to be so fucked. Her braids are coming undone and I tell her that I will tighten them up for her. That makes Layla Jackson stop crying. She says, And to top it off, Rakeem is a shit. He promised me he wouldn't say nothing but now that he's back in school he is broadcasting my shit all over the place. And that makes nobody like me. And that makes nobody want to touch me.

I put my arm around Layla. Soon her crying stops and she is thinking about something else.

But me, I know these new words and the old words without looking at them, without the dictionary, without Ma's hands on my head. Lasheema and Tata come in and want their hair to be like Layla's and they bring in the Vaseline and sit around my feet like shoes. Tommy wakes up still in sleep and shouts, Lula, get your ass on in here. Then he falls back to sleep.

Because I know I will always be able to say the words on my own. I can do the words on my own and that is what matters. I have this flavor of the pie and I will always have it. Here in this kitchen I was always safe, learning the words till my eyes hurt. The words are in my heart.

Ma comes in and shoves Lula Jean into a kitchen chair. She says, Kids, make room for your cousin, go in the other room and tell Tommy to get his lame ass out here. Layla, you can get your ass out of here and don't bring it back no more with this child sick out his mind, do your 'ho'ing somewhere out on the street where you belong. Tommy, since when I need to tell you how to treat your wife? You are a stupid heel. Learn how to be a man.

Everybody leaves and Ma changes.

She says, I ain't forgot that special dinner for you, baby. I'm glad you're safe and sound here with me. Let's practice later.

I tell her, Okay, Ma, but I got to go meet Rakeem first.

She looks at me in shock and then out the corner of my eye I can tell she wants me to say no, I'll stay, I won't go to him. Because she knows.

But I'm getting my coat on and Ma has got what will be tears on her face because she can't say no and she can't ask any questions. Keep moving.

And I am thinking of Rocky's Pizza and how I will be when I get there and how I will be when I get home. Because I am coming back home. And I am going to school tomorrow. I know the words, and I can tell them to Rakeem and I can share what I know. Now he may be ready. I want him to say to me in his mind: Please give me a chance. And I know that behind Rocky's Pizza is the only place where I don't have to keep moving. Where there is not just air in me that keeps me from crumbling, but blood and meat and strong bones and feelings. I will be me for a few minutes behind Rocky's Pizza and I don't care if it's just a few minutes. I pat my hair down in the mirror next to the kitchen door. I take Anita's letter knife out my jacket pocket and leave it on the table next to where Tommy is standing telling his wife that she never knew what love was till she met him and why does she have to be like that, talking about leaving him and shit? You keep going that way and you won't ever know how to keep a man, bitch.

country of the
spread out god

TAMMY

On my way to making breakfast, I tell her that I remember
good. Auntie snaps at me, A dat Ah raise yuh far? How dare
yuh remember *good* is all yuh deserve to remember is de
hexact opposite: *baaad*. She snaps, How yuh so brash dese
days, yuh is deserve remembarance a what coulda been and
den ache when yuh realize. Ain't no new morning coming.
You leavin de family wid yuh head. Yuh deserve *bad,* yuh
deserve *orrible*. This is all Auntie snapping at me. I only
see her once a year when she comes here on her shopping
spree for all the Jamaicans left behind. December, January,
etc. equals peaceful for me. Auntie comes in June to Jersey
City. The ones left behind, they all know of me and hate
me dearly. Uncles, cousins, and other secondhand relatives.
When Auntie comes back to Longwood, South Bronx, she
goes and shakes down the golden legends: how when she was
living here full-time and caring for us she raised us as best as
she could; Bad Neighborhood; how she tried to blossom me;
A Truly Strong Influence; Kids not what dey was in de ol
daze. How she tried to mek mi mind shoot. *Ah Tammy, fe
true.* I listen to her. I get the feeling of legends, something

like twenty miles with no shoes in the burning desert, the infectious jungle, and back. A long hard journey. The people back home, they hear the stories, they wish me dead. The last words out of her mouth are, Don't is yuh let me hear yuh mention again *good,* cause if yuh do, well den. *Hamassi.*

I am gettin ready fe di pool, Auntie. Me want to swim and swim and swim lacka got a place to shine. I got dis feelin, Auntie, lacka chuch belief, lacka someting strong, me man gone kill me today, Auntie. Dat how much him loves me. I got to get me swimming, it me chuch. I stroke. Watah splashin me and savin me. But I gotta do dat befo mi darlin boy he kill me dead cause him does love me.

She ignores my language laid out just for her and cuts her eye teeth and goes on to tell me that for fifteen years when she was here in Longwood, South Bronx, she tried to be a mother, like I was now trying, but that unlike me, she cared too much, and that's how she got to the hole where she is today, and how would I understand being in a hole, just how, when I was so free with my ways? So free. She says all these years she didn't mind being at the bottom of the heap so long as her babies were okay, but here we are, look at us, me sixteen and Rob fourteen years old, and it's enough to shame a person fe life. *Good* don't mean a thing. *Good* gone. Clouds promise rain but deliver a flood. You never did anything to deserve that kind of treatment but here it is. Flood. Even at the bottom of the heap, flood.

She looks over and maybe she wants to put her arms around me, but then the thought smacks her dead in the center of her memory, and she informs me that I am no longer kin to her. She tells me, Tis justice yu pain me so? And den turn aroun and remember *good* while I here in de mos miserable sufferin known possible to mankind? Auntie's singsong voice from back home is a bouquet of flowers that aren't from these parts. They bloom all year long, but especially hard in Longwood, South Bronx. They open wide, fruity, and poisonous.

This isn't the first time. I have heard it all before, only worse. And I know I don't have to take this kind of thing. Right now, after all these years, I am too busy tending to the garden of my self-esteem, and I know I don't have to take this kind of thing. Everywhere I turn, every day, I learn how much I am a bed of roses, of gorgeous orange tiger lilies and cake-smelling freesia. Frangipani, bougainvillea, lady-of-the-night. And after I go swimming today, I never want to leave my apartment again. I used to go swimming at the Blue Danube Pool, but after today I am all over that. I want him to kill me. I want him to care enough to want to kill me. Here, in this room. The way the moon shines on my room at night, on me and the kid's clothes hanging on the backs of the chairs and glistening, percolating. The way the moon keeps us safe. I never want to leave.

The phone rings and it's his sister, Jean. Now she is on my back, wanting to know why I left the kid over at hers so early in the morning, and if Rob is okay, and why after all these years, why, when we were like brother and sister, family practically, why did after all these years I go and do a thing like that. It's an old question. I can tell Jean is going to try and break up my garden.

Who dat on de phone, Auntie asks me. I don't give an answer. Pretty soon she can hear the loud voice over the other end, and so she rolls her eyes, remembering how she worked hard to raise Rob and me. Bottom of the heap.

And I look out the window and there come Sleepy and Rob and two other Potential Thugs strolling down the street as if it were not just a sunny beautiful Sunday morning without a cloud in the sky but also a good day to break up something. From my window I can see them head up to our building. The cement is cracked in places, but that is good, because then flowers can secretly be born there and surprise us when we are walking out the house, on our way to somewhere, most likely angry at some assorted thing or other, and then we look down and notice this little flower stretching its little head out and calling at us in flower talk to look down and wonder at its prettiness. And we are forced to look down then, and all of a sudden we realize that the world can unfold for you.

Sleepy kicks in the door while the two Potential Thugs, really seventh-grade boys in their grown sisters' old leather jackets, jump into the living room and start looking all around, pushing furniture out the way, opening doors, even picking up the framed pictures on the television console and examining them carefully. Rob hunches into the kitchen and yells, "Where's the Little Man? Don't tell me you're not going to tell me where is the Little Man?" and he hits the coffeepot off the stove with a new baseball bat.

Auntie says in a plain voice, "When head buck yuh, yuh cyan trus forehead."

I put one hand on my hip and use the fingers on the other hand to twirl the curls in my hair that I just pressed in this morning. Rob doesn't like it that I am taking time out to think. So he starts to bat the refrigerator in, and he has made a dent in it the size of a head. You know what I'm talking about.

Sleepy runs in with a baby blanket. His face is on fire, something I have never seen on him because you don't get a name for nothing after all, and it is like a cop show, like a camera somewhere is getting all the moves and will later ask him to do the same thing in another house where the mother is holding out on the father, trying to hide the kids from their own flesh and blood.

I finally say, before Rob decides to go back to his old ways and hit me, I say, "The kid is over at your sister's. Why do you have to mash in a perfectly good refrigerator? If the kid was here, don't you think he would get scared or something? Why is it that after all these years, I am still at the bottom of the heap? Tell me, you asshole, what can I do to *not* be at the bottom of the heap?"

But Rob is already on the phone to Jean. Auntie looks at me like a wasted cat. She says this is the last time I will see her. Her suitcases are packed.

She has done all she can. She has worked and she has slaved. Auntie's hair is up in a fifties-style big puff on top of her head, and her dress is tight and cuts off right below the knees. Her shoes are soft princess slippers from the old country and her skin is like a smooth green fig. She left us last year. She be done wid us.

Auntie's hair bobs. She says, "Yu doan worry. Jesus is mi judge. I av mi passport." Rob says, "Thank God for that."

And me, I have all these people in my house acting like animals, because everybody is selfish about their own something and they are all pissed to see all the other somethings that live in the world today and are taking up *their* space and *their* breathing air and *their* room for mercy, and I think it's a miracle that I can remember *good* at all in the face of all this. Don't you? I was on my way to making breakfast.

Rob takes the baseball bat and lays it on the table. I'm this close, he says, and he waits another moment, I see something taper in his brain, and then he picks the bat up and combs the air with it, back and forth, toward my head.

On this miserable Sunday morning, before Rob comes over, I am in the kitchen with my auntie, who is looking at some baby booties she is knitting and unraveling, humming her old pain stories, the old ancient sweat of Rob on my nightgown that I haven't washed in weeks and me trying to be my own garden and I am trying to concentrate on what for breakfast.

But all along in my head, here are the *good* memories. His curly hair, *good*. His missing-tooth grin, *good*. His brown velvet skin with baby oil on it, *good*. The time he came into our house and Auntie said, "Dis beeny bwoy be stayin' wid us from nowwon, so yuh all beeehaave," *good*. The fact that he was only seven years old but could say things like "I'm still a little kid, so what do you expect me to say?" and really mean it, and we would all burst out laughing because who in their right mind knows how to say that beginning *then?*

The smell of his body when he was asleep with me in my bed, *good*. The way he said he never had no family before and now he had one and that's why he can't stop crying, *good*. The shirt he made in sewing class for me, *good*. The time he let me dress him up in my cheerleader's uniform, *good*. The way his face looked when he was twelve, thirteen, thirteen and a half. The new smell of his man's body, *good*.

The time when I was in the hospital and was crying out his name, only his name, not Auntie's, which made her mad as hell. It was just his name, and he heard me, from all the way in our house he heard me, it was like a psychedelic love connection, and in it he rode his bike over to see me, just in time for the baby's head to bloom out from between my legs, he was probably walking into the waiting room, and the nurse was probably running after him saying, "No one under sixteen allowed in that waiting room!" He heard me, *good*.

Then the time, way back, when he and I were playing find-the-stick, and I found it, only he didn't want me to find it, and then he didn't want to admit that I found it, so he punched me in my face, gentle. So I hit him back, then we were rolling on the floor, and Auntie came in and said, "Cho! What carryin-awns!" and tried to separate us, but that didn't work, so she left, and I kept slapping him, and his tears turned to laughs, and he just belted me one more time in the stomach, and then we stopped and there was a need to kiss each other and make up. We said just like Auntie O God O God Look Down on Us Lost for our prayers and made up, so when Auntie arrived with the man from next door, Mr. Home, he was supposed to break up our out-of-hand kiddie fight, we just shouted, "There's no need for you, Mr. Home, so why don't you just scram back on home?" and that was so hysterical. Auntie apologized and didn't speak to us or cook for us in three days. She didn't appreciate the kissing. She said to us, "I doan recinnize yu brash debbils," and that was also hysterical to us. Because we knew the word was "re-*cog*-nize." *Good.*

ROB

I am a friend first. And Sleepy always been my main hanging buddy. Always. Rain or shine. Rain or shine.

Most of the time it was me and Sleepy alone. It was something special, I can't right explain it. Me and him in the fourth grade, fifth, or hanging by the swings till it got way late and I was in trouble. Seventh grade. He kept me by his side in all unfortunate mishaps and disturbances of a fighting nature, and we didn't have to look each other in the eye. I knew what he meant, and it made me have these special feelings. Volcano lava hot heat desert sun. These feelings.

Sleepy and I observed the same girls in school, but he was the only one who actually got to say, "Can I do *you?*" Me, I was just looking. I didn't have that effect. There was one though, I seen her in Mrs. Rodriguez' class, only she wouldn't look at me, she being a Spanish girl. She wouldn't check out my shit, being that I was only fourteen and all, but then when I saw her in Family Court, I said, "Oh God Oh God Look Down on Us Lost!" and she heard me, and she laughed when I told her I was lost in her beauty, and one thing led naturally to another. She was sixteen, and before she wouldn't check out my shit, me a fourteen-year-old nigga and all, I wasn't what she would call choice. But then I seen her in Family Court. Jesus helped me. You could say we made an acquaintance.

Sleepy said, "Go for what you want. Attain that peak. You a man in a man's world." He dug the Spanish girls, especially the big ones where every damn thing is hanging out. Their meat was tender, and they knew how to preserve a man, was Sleepy's philosophy.

Me, I tried to rap the rap, but then the Gorilla Girl finds out through her spiderweb network in Mrs. DeJesus' class, and she shoves her finger all up in my face and says, "You think it's gonna be that way? Well you got another thing coming!" Then she takes in a whole lot of breath. She says, "Remember *that* baby waiting home with your sister Jean? Well, you better fucking remember it cause you're the father. *You are the father.* This ain't no dream you can walk out from when you see something new!" And she is proud because she sees the frozenness in my face. I just sit there on the playground swings. She folds her arms over her chest. Proud. Everybody's making noise round me, everybody's life just seems to go on and on and my life is not even a grain of fucking sand compared to theirs. It is not a grain.

So Sleepy comes up and whispers in my ear, "Hey, Lourdes says she's yours tonight, if you want it like that," but then the Gorilla is there to say, "You better wipe that fucking look off your fucking face."

I was only seven before. The caretaker from St. Jude's came by my mom's place and didn't approve and said I was going to live in a new place. And it was pretty nice. It had building blocks to play with, and a nurse came round all the time and told me I was so cute, she wished she could take me home with her because she didn't have any children of her own, and I was so cute.

But then my auntie came to get me. And she was sort of cheerful, and sort of light. She looked Spanish, but I knew she was black. So we head on to her house. My sister Jean was shipped to Auntie's sister Geraldine the nun over in Jamaica, the old country. She said it was too hot. Then she came back to live on her own in Longwood, South Bronx. By then she was old enough to say or think whatever the hell she wanted. Sixteen.

Me, I had to share the room with Tammy, but right as soon as I get there, she says, "I'm afraid, please sleep next to me," because she was only nine years old, and right after that, she tells me to call her Gorilla Girl cause she has the strength of ten men all in her little finger, and she wants to wrestle me to sleep.

TAMMY

I was a swimmer. I first got the idea to swim from the night in the hospital, right before I felt my water creeping up on me. I had a baby swimming somewhere in me, and I was like the ocean. And at the same time I was keeping the baby afloat, drifting in my pool, swimming to find the way out, and there it was, a large hole that you didn't have trouble finding and on the outside of it was sparkling light, and out popped his little head, and the first thing I did was turn to Auntie and say, "I'm naming him Little Rob," and she turns her face from exaltation to a question mark and then to an angry flicker and she says right there in front of the doctor, "What yuh *mean* Little Rob is he ain't de fadder!" and the doctor is busy wiping the blood from the screaming body who is declaring, "I made it out the pool! I made it out the pool!" and there wasn't anything left for Auntie to do but think a minute more and let that flicker work its way deeper into her chest and then she fainted dead away. The nurse woke her up. I was holding Little Rob in my arms and saying, "I'ma love you, I'ma care for you, there's not a thing you got to worry about," and the nurse was sighing, "I just *love* to watch the bond between a mother and a child." Auntie had to leave the room. She walked into the waiting pavilion with her scrubs.

There she seen Rob. She said to him, "Yuh boat like one flesh, bredda and sis. Hamassi!" Which means Lord Have Mercy in the old talk. Then she fainted.

Rob was allowed in. The nurse introduced him as my brother because that was what he had told her, that was the only way he thought he could get in to see me, only if he was my blood-related family. I passed the baby into his arms. There was a halo over his shiny round head. He whispered, "Tell me, Tammy, is it mines?" It was such a beautiful moment, one I will always reminisce on. Because one day I will be old, and maybe I will be in Auntie's place, and I will know that things will only get worse. I looked at him standing there in the warm hospital light and I said, "What you think, stupid?" and he just took my smile for something special. It was one of those moments not for words. *I* wasn't going to give him words. It was me for him and him for me and the baby. We're gonna move outa here and start a new life somewheres so I can prove to you that I am a man and you can prove to me that you are a real woman.

At least it was that way till he started to want that Spanish chick at school. Then I had to take what you call drastic measures. I dragged his ugly immature ass to Family Court. You think one thing, but it's really another.

He was there in the hallway day before yesterday, Friday, waiting to appear before our usual Judge Chalmers, a white lady who has feelings for girls like me. She once said to me, "Look at where I am today. You can do it too, Tammy."

He glanced up at me, and that was the first time I had the

feeling that I was doing something bad. Like, I was the culprit, the villain, I was the only thing standing in between him and true happiness. His eyes were pointy, like a cat's. He was holding his math book, and I felt ashamed of him still trying to pass sixth-grade math. And the fact that this was the fourth day in a row for his pants, you could see the bicycle grease from Sleepy's old bike on the calves, but hey, it's like I always say: When you have a kid and you like showing him off in the finest, you got to sacrifice something.

In fact, that's the first thing he says to me. He says, "What happened to Little Man's French L'Amour sweatshirt? I thought I told you to put the French L'Amour on him today for court." He is pointing to the baby boy I have on my hip.

I say, "Hey, shithead, you think you can talk to me that way?" Because this is how I let him know I still love him.

He says, "Fuck you, Tammy. I ain't taking this shit anymore. Don't tell me you're my family anymore. I got my whole life in front of me. Fuck you, Tammy." And he closes his book because he notices I been staring at it. And he fixes his eyes on the gray tile floor, right outside the courtroom with Judge Chalmers sitting in it.

I jump up and say, "Oh yeah? Well you can go fuck yourself, Rob."

He jumps right back in my face. "Fuck you two more times than that, Tammy Cocksucker."

I swing the baby in front of me. I say, "Fuck you into infinity, Rob. And by the way, this ain't your kid."

He smacks me in the face and makes my chin hit the top of the baby's head. He says, "You want to say that again, bitch?"

I say, "This ain't yours, boy! You ain't got the juice!"

He starts laughing and pushes my head with his hand. He does it again. He says, "Don't be shitting me, bitch. You know how I get when you start shitting me."

I say, "Where were you on the night of August twentieth, 1984? Hell, I don't recall you being by my way. You better get out of here."

He laughs and makes like he is going to slap me. But he doesn't. We wait a minute. Then he says, "Next time, don't have my kid coming here looking like a public assistance baby. You got clothes for him. I pay for French L'Amour. Don't make me come and have to teach you a lesson." And we walk into the courtroom, a family, with his arm around my shoulder.

ROB

It's at another one of those points. A low point when I sit on the rail on Bruckner Expressway and look down. Can I go on this journey? Sometimes I ask myself, Can I make it on this journey anymore? It's not my usual frame of thinking, because I'm usually with Sleepy and the boys, but sometimes a man has to find himself in the lion's pit before he can call himself a man.

This Spanish girl is like an angel. I see her at Family Court. She speaks to me. She doesn't give me a lot of details, but she does tell me that she's not there because of herself but because of her sister, her sister's baby's father ain't acting like a man, delusions, etc. There's a little boy that follows Lourdes around and puts his head behind her legs but she says that's her little brother. So I fascinate my eyes on her. I love this angel. We find a minute and sit down on one of those benches and we conversate. It's when I'm sure that the Gorilla has already left for swimming. And I'm thanking the fucking Lord that she is underwater somewhere.

And it's not any foolishness being talked here. No. This girl is special. I can feel it. This is the one. She has everything I've been yearning for. I look at her and I tell her with my eyes, "Come to me mine."

Do you know what it's like to suddenly feel like everything around you has been in vain, and now life has a whole new meaning? When you look back on all your long years and realize that it has been a waste and you ain't done anything at all?

I got my kid, and I'm never gonna lose him. I don't care where Tammy tries to hide him, I'm always gonna find my blood. He's really young. He's at that delicate stage. That impressionable stage in a child's development. What he takes in now, that will undoubtedly affect him for the rest of his life. Auntie reminds me of that every fucking time I see her come from Jamaica. You have to be careful when it comes to raising children. They are our future.

Now this Spanish girl, Lourdes, I love the way her ass looks in this one summer dress, but now she tells me all about the Dominican Republic, and how summery it is there, and how you can eat the fruit off the trees, mango, tamarind, fig, almond, and you can be filled up for the day. How the river is clean enough to drink and wash your clothes in. That's the place I want to be. Land of the tame wild animal, land of the peaceful night sky, land of the dreaming trees, like she says. Country of the Spread Out God. He don't leave nothing out. This Spread Out God with black arms and cloud pillows for hands. Everyone is taken care of. Every corner, every window. Lourdes with pale skin and Spanish eyes and a passion tongue. Her mouth is tasty to me. A little salt, a little sweet. And I think: This is the Opportunity. Sleepy is behind me, 100 percent. He says I owe it to myself. Get free. Go for the Opportunity of Happiness Supreme.

TAMMY

Thursday I see him in the street riding Sleepy's bike. I call out, "Hey you asshole, when you coming by to see me?" and he looks at me and keeps right on moving. He's been staying

33

with Sleepy over at Booba's house and his calls don't come too much. I see him up the street a little ways ahead and I shout, "Hey asshole!" and at that point he says, "Keep your ugly-ass shirt on. I'll try and swing by tonight," and then three days go by.

ROB

I'm not proud of the fact. Don't think for a minute that I'm proud of that fact. Family Court is one of the worst drags a man, or even a woman, can go through. All that sitting and waiting. You realize that you really are in the armpit of hell when you are waiting in Family Court.

Don't misbelieve me. I love my kid. When I'm not with Sleepy, my kid's on my mind like a crown. But the rule in life that I am busy learning right now is: Don't let them see you sweat. Don't let them in on your goodness.

My kid and my man Sleepy. He's the man. He's the only man for me. These feelings, ain't nobody ever cared for me like he has done. Sleepy got my back, my front, and all the sides of me covered. Where would I be without him? He's even in my fucking dreams. I start crying in bed, and I don't want to hold on to Tammy no more, my holding feelings for her is gone with the wind, and so there's this picture of Sleepy in my mind that carries me over the threshold and walks me into the Valley of Light. I can breathe in his brave skin. He's not only a friend, he's a man. What is it, in me, *for him?*

TAMMY

I can remember *good.* When Rob and me first said we was going to do it, we waited till Auntie was sound asleep. And it was so fun, tricking Auntie like that. But we were both feeling like it was time for the man and woman in us to emerge.

So we did it, and at first I was like, "So this is it?" and Rob was like, "No, I am supposed to put it in your hole, like this, only you won't hold still," and I said, "A *real* man would know what to do, Robby." So he smacked me, right there in the twin bed, and he said he *was* a real man, and did I want to be permanently fixed so's I wouldn't know the pleasures of a man ever again, and then Auntie came into the bedroom and said, "Why is yuh two fightin at dis hower?" but we just told her to go on back to bed, wasn't anything she needed to concern herself about. Rob said, "Auntie, I don't know what you suggesting, but I am only a child," and we laughed, and Auntie said, "Waal, I doan wan no foolishness. Let a ol lady ave some peace to dream in."

But back in the night, Rob told me to stay right there, so I stayed right there and he told me to push, so I pushed. He said, "There is supposed to be blood here, how come you ain't bleeding?" and I said, "Rob, how am I supposed to know *how?*"

So here we are keeping on trying to make my hole bleed. When I am doing the butterfly in the pool, I remember that night. It was the first time. It was like breaking out of the nut of loneliness that has been suffocating you for so many years.

When I am swimming at the Blue Danube Pool, I make long water-sweeping movements. I make short punches. I make the water dance under my belly, swoon in my hair. The Breakthrough Crawl is my own invention. The back flips over, and it's all about this sudden spurt of happiness that happens in your body at the moment when you think everything is pure shit, and the joy lifts you up higher and higher, and your head goes in and out, in and out of the water. It takes a whole lot of breath to do the Breakthrough Crawl. Auntie came to watch me one afternoon from the special parents section at the Blue Danube and when it was over, she said, "Rock-stone a ribber bottom never feel sun-hot." The lifeguard at the Blue Danube always says to me, "Honey, if we could get all the girls here to do like you, well then I don't know what."

ROB

So my last appointment at Family Court was last Friday. Sleepy slugged me on the arm outside the courthouse, and then he said, "Solid." I went in.

I wasn't thinking anything in particular. The Gorilla was there, telling Judge Chalmers how I was a unfit father, how she really needs the money, especially if I am thinking of the Dominican Republic, and how I was terrorizing just about near everybody, a unfit father, and of course that made the manly pride in myself rise up. I don't need St. Jude's to tell me to act like a man. Look around you. Everyone who I need to know, they know I am acting a man.

So Judge Chalmers gives me this lecture and I say, "Yes ma'am I promise that I will do better I will get a job yes I know what is responsibility no I am not just a machine I am a thinking human being with a heart too." And such bullshit as I always tell her. She makes me hand over my last twenty bucks, and then there's all the papers I have to sign, and the priest is there from St. Jude's and he puts his arms around me and says, "You know, Robert Lee, we could get you into some after-school program like your friend Tammy. Do you know that she has been teaching the younger children how to swim? She is the best in water safety. Did you ever think she could turn around so much?" And it is obvious that this old man has been shitted over big-time by her. He thinks she is just a friend I knocked up. Not the nuns, though. The nuns are in on that mess. They just tell me, "Don't fly in the face of the Lord, young man. He will take all your joy away one day. Which is His Everlasting Mercy and Redemption." And the same similar bullshit.

But soon the priest lets me go, and who should I see when I get out in the corridor but this dream Spanish girl, Lourdes, and she is waiting outside another courtroom, and when I ask her about her sister, she says, "Who?" But I skip over that. We look into each other's eyes. She says, "I want to tell you more about the Dominican Republic, but it doesn't look like I'm going there no time soon," and this doesn't bother me one bit. I sit next to her. I smell the honey-comb perfume on her neck. I want to bite it like an ant, but instead I sit and listen to stories of the old home. Auntie has told me about the ants that climb into the flowers and suck out the juice. This girl is an absolute dream, damn straight. With her we are all saved.

I bring along this baseball bat. It's a beautiful Sunday day early morning wind and coldness in your throat. I want to change things. I want to take Little Man and change things. I want to give love. I am clear.

I see the Gorilla acting calm in the kitchen, and I don't want to hear or feel her breathe anymore. I used to hit her. But now I don't want to go into all that. I just don't want her breath anymore. Sometimes it's so loud and broiling that my ears crack. Sometimes I miss her strong arms to handle a man.

TAMMY

It's early, before what is to come. I'm on my way to making Sunday morning breakfast for me and Auntie before she leaves me for good. This is the last time. She is getting ready to leave with her big suitcases full of department store stuff that will get wrapped up in plastic at the airport. She says she wishes she could see her Robbie one more time before she goes, talk some sense. She wishes she could see Robbie and hold his baby in her arms one more time. And other fairy tales. I look out the window. Soon he will be up this sidewalk. He is on his way.

Eggs scrambled with peppers and onions and a little guava jelly on the side. She eats slowly, like there's just one more thing before she goes. I say goodbye to her in my mind. Then it hits me. I am getting the mugs out the cupboard, and I have this hankering for Rob's flesh. I would like to hold him tonight. Just us in the apartment. I want him to start thinking about the old days again. I wouldn't mind if we had a fistfight in the kitchen. I wouldn't mind at all if he slugged me in the chest, or if we fell laughing into each other's arms and then wrestled ourselves to safety. That floor is always a nice place to wind up in a sex reconciliation. I wouldn't mind. After that you dream in your sleep.

don't erase me

FOR DORIS JEAN AUSTIN

APRIL 28, 1993

Gain some weight. Gain fifty pounds. Find somebody to cook dinner for. Don't just make vegetables, don't follow that Slim Dream Plan, the one you been on since you were a young fat girl. Make plantains. Molasses-fried pork chops. Cherry dump cake. Corncob supreme. Get rid of the diet pills. You were born fat, and now the sickness makes you want more fat, more all over so you'll stay longer. Read the newspaper. Find out what's going on in the world. Find out if someone somewhere is experimenting. Find out if their hope is for real, not just to shut mouths. Press your hair. Turn the ends blond. Go to the black people's college in Brooklyn. Learn something before you go. Do it behind everyone's back. They never had a lot of trust in you, but show them that you have it for yourself. Call the center: are they sure about what to do when you finally pass? Do they have your mother's name in writing? What is passing like? Is a home in the clouds such a stupid thing to believe in? And what does it really mean, *inconclusive?* What is the damn point of telling people a word like that? Because that word there *is* a lie. Be up-front with folks. No one got nowhere else to go at this point.

Buy a miniskirt on sale at Wowow's that can do the right thing. Show it to the man you're cooking for. Send the kids to their grandmother. Get her to get used to them. Because pretty soon they will have to call her Granny whether she likes it or not. Can't be the fountain of youth forever. Call the phone company. Ask them just for incoming calls. You can't afford otherwise. Get people to call you. You can be a friend still. Wash the piss out the children's drawers.

Return to your moms. Think about how you can get her to return to you. She once was like that, do you recall? Tender. But you: don't *you* go down in flames. She will be one of those who complain at the top of their voice, "I shoulda, I shoulda, what was wrong with me — *then*?" But you, just *you* don't go down in flames.

Ask the person you're cooking dinner for what he thinks about the future. Tell him, "Whatever it takes." You'll be there. Tell him your dreams. You made it this far. He can count on you to be there for a while at least. No fear.

Call the center and tell them you're coming back, but in your own time. Get their hot-line number just in case. But tell them you ain't coming back anytime soon, only when you are ready to feel the universe in your hands, your feet. You can lead your life any way you want for the rest of the time you got. They are not God. Stop your crying. Stop those kids crying. The doctor checked them out. They are a miracle. They are okay. Gain weight fast. Call the person who put their arms around you one afternoon when it thundered and lightninged and said, "If you ever need someone." Need someone.

Write it down so there's more than just a name and a picture of you left for them. Write the whole frikkin story down. It doesn't matter if they cry later. Let em. Go backwards. Write the whole shit down backwards in memory so it will make them see *all* the points along the way, make them say, "Was that me? How hard, how hard I was." Write the entire masterpiece down. Let them try. Let them try. But hell. When you get down to it, right down to it, they can never know, not like you.

Rebirth yourself. They can never know like you.

APRIL 27, 1993

In my red wallpapered apartment, back on Brook Avenue. This used to be the place where I planned for my family to come together and start correctly. Only now Stepfather Bridge comes in the kitchen where I am cooking and says, This all wouldn't a happened if you had just let nature take its natrul course. I'm for you. Why can't you be for me. Why you push me away. When will people just learn things are not always what they seem. The early bird was in my hand. God put me on this earth for a reason. That's you.

While I am cooking my herbal broth I say, I don't care if your ass is all alone now. That's what you deserve. Shit. And you are not going to have me in your corner. You're on your damn own.

He says, No one is deserving of that kind of unforgiveness.

Then he says, after he sees me sit down and breathe heavy, like he believes I'm going to keel over any minute, he says, Even I forgave you. You made me sick, and I forgave you. Let me back in. I just want to be back in.

I am sitting on my bed. These days the tiredness makes me plain sad. I used to could clean my whole house on my own and then go walk in the street. That was the old days. When I am in my own place, what should have been for me and Ty and the kids, and I make vegetable broth or farina at the stove, then the pain in the area above my vagina hurts, it bowls me down, and I have to sit, and I ache remembering all the things I used to could do standing up. I hate seeing this man in front of me. He was the first time I had sex. Years later, after I found out it was true for me, he said he wouldn't have the test done, he knew it couldn't be true for him. Was it evil to wish it could be true for him? I never used to care about a home in the clouds.

I say, You never were in. And you made *me* sick.

He says, Let me love you the way we used to love each other. I don't want in your body no more. You made *me* sick. I just am tired of being alone.

My moms kicked him out. Finally after all these years.

I say, I have better than you.

I tell him before I throw up a little in my cup, Ain't nobody going to remember you when you're gone, old man. Love is more than surviving.

Then I say, Now get your ass on outta here. You the one making me sick.

The sky was striped with yellow. The people was going on just as usual. The sidewalk had cracks with garbage in them, and love was on everybody's mind.

And what Stepfather Bridge doesn't know is that my horizon is stretched out in front of me like a long black limousine.

JANUARY 23, 1993
I see you looking at me. Not you. *You.* Your big bad devilish handsome bowlegged fine self. I'm not generally for big-muscle types, but hey, you all right. Check me out. Yes, I'm all woman. One hundred and ten percent. Come on over. I think you are sweet to look at. Don't make excuses. This here's the only beer I'm having. I know what I see.

Yes. I love the way you are to me. The feel of your tongue tip tenderizing my ear. No one has ever made me feel that way before. I didn't think it would be possible.

.   .   .

Are we still together? How long do you have? Don't ask me how long do I have, I'm not into counting the days. Life is meant to be lived. I'm not no superwoman, neither. There are times when I really have to lie down, or sleep, or whatever, just stop going. In the end, it's you and the Maker figuring the plan, and sometimes you really don't have a say about any damn thing.

Are we still together? Tell me you dig me one more time. Don't just whisper it in my ear, *shout it.* Then let me stroke your silky black beard till I am convinced now and forever that this is no nightmare.

JUNE 27, 1992
I'm throwing a party for me and my babies and anybody else who feels like coming. I'm very easy. You can bring guests if you feel like it. It's in my new apartment, red wallpaper with yellow roses swimming through the creases. Mott Haven Avenue near the precinct, the one for me and my family. Or you can come alone. You can drink all the vodka in this room. Or you can bring up some beer. It's my party, hey.

I'm going to be playing some dope music and Aunt Nay-Nay said she would do the cooking so you know what that means! She is always there for you. Have you ever known anybody like that in your life? And there will also be some good, loving, slow-jamming music. I got that on my mind too. There's no reason a man couldn't come in and slow-jam with me.

Delicious eats, vodka from Russia, orange soda and ice, and no curfew. There ain't no reason for anybody to be lonely this night.

And any person who wants to stay the whole time with me, well that's just fine. Hey *you.* The fine one with the pretty face and Chinese eyes. Do you like me? We been talking for a while. It's my party. Only happiness is allowed.

MARCH 15, 1992
So I went down to the center all the way in Manhattan and I came back home to the Bronx. A cloudy green day with no letting up in sight. I think God always knows precisely what he is doing, so there is no reason to ever question. Moms called me on the phone soon as I stepped in the door. I was feeling wiped. I sat in my chair by the sink and let the phone ring. And all the time I was thinking: There ain't no reason people will look at me differently. They already know I'm not special or anything. They knew that from before. No reason to look at me now.

I got up about a half-hour later and picked up the phone. It was Moms who said, Don't tell me no bad news. Remember the Lord is there to listen. The Lord has the strength to listen. I'm just a mortal woman, nothing but dust on a meaty frame. Just a weak servant of the Father.

I said, Your grandchildren are going to need you when I am gone.

She hung up the phone. No, she slammed it down, let's not get cute now. When she called back a few seconds later, it sounded like she was throwing up, like she was having morning sickness again. I had to think of the day I moved out her place, when I was tossing all my things into a little pink suitcase that had once belonged to an old dolly of mine, it was her travel case for her dresses and attachments, only now I was heading out this loony bin once and for all. Some people were good at driving stakes. My stepfather Bridge was saying, You're breaking our hearts. And when that didn't work, he said, You're taking the life outta your mama, girl, bring your ass back on in here. And that just made me start working faster to get the hell out. I took the radio on the dresser he bought me in the beginning when he didn't think I would tell my moms he was feeling on me. He tried to stop me. But I swung the radio at him and let him know that suddenly I got strong. Even if that meant I was all alone. Bullshit was not accepted here no more.

So now Moms calls back and she's heaving on the phone and talking about the Lord and why couldn't I just tell Him my problems and why did it always have to be *mothers* who received the worst amount of pain? All kinds of crazy shit like that. *Hello out there!* I am a mother too, but she conveniently forgot about that fact. You can't tell a mother how to act.

And then she yelled at me, didn't I ever want to do anything with my future? Then she called me a selfish so-and-so. Then she asked me didn't I ever want to have kids, real ones, with a man who was my legitimate husband? Kids who I could better myself for? Then she told me not to expect her to be taking care of Tee and Charlene later. She was still young. Forty-two was not too old to start a new family of her own. She had lots of living left to do. Couldn't be bothered with selfish shit.

I don't let a minute of quiet dredge between us. I tell her that the doctor told me that I would have to start taking good care of myself now. He gave me the names of the vitamins I would need, different ones than the ones I had been taking. And I would have to start with prescription medicine at some point. And that it was better to know now than wait and get worse off.

I ask my moms if she's listening. She answers, No.

I say, The doctor at the center was really nice to me. He didn't turn away. And he was also really cute.

She says, Surely your head can't be thinking of those kinds of things now.

I say, They gave me my results and they were kind of expecting me to cry. But I told them, no, I ain't sweating it.

It's not all that much of a surprise. I've had worse things to deal with.

Moms says, Oh really? What is worse than one day ending up a shame-filled corpse? And then they won't bury you, ever think of that, Miss Smart-Ass? They will refuse to put your shame-filled body into the earth. Ain't that going to be the death of me?

I say, Moms, tell me the truth. You know too much. You been reading up on things.

She screams, No I have not! Fool, selfish fool.

I say, I am planning a new life.

She says, You could make me proud. You could take a course at Medgar Evers College in Brooklyn. You could do one good thing in your life. Selfish fool.

The list goes on.

Night

It's better to know than to not know. It's better to know than to not know. It's better to know than to not know. I keep on crying even though I have this plain fact in front of me.

JANUARY 4, 1992

There is this girl I watch. She doesn't let nothing get in her way. Maybe she knows she'll always be in people's minds, and maybe that keeps her going. Her mother doesn't worry if she wears her nightgown in the street over some pants or if she goes out without finishing her hair. She'll have the front half of her head all greased down and shit, permed, and the back half is all out, straight, linty, just a comb in it that means: I'm on my damn own. The other day I heard her in the street saying: You got a problem with that? I dare you to say you got a problem. The boy in her face just shook his head and handed her over twenty bucks.

This girl, her name is Melody. I been knowing her since I

was a child. First I lived with my mother and my stepfather. Then my stepfather came after me in dreams. Then in reality. Then my uncle Billy from Princeton, New Jersey, stepped in and broke my stepfather's jaw and went to prison. He had been the only one on my side. He still brags to this day about the feel of face bone in your hands. So I moved out on my own.

Melody on the street, they say she has a bona fide college degree. The street bugged out when it first heard that. But it is true. She went to Oklahoma to a university. It's what someone said. She was studying history or something that made her ask a lot of questions about black people, *her* people. She calls out the names all the time. Harriet Tubman: feeling the moss on the north side of the trees. Thurgood Marshall: never gave up even when spit in the face. Stokely Carmichael: leader and beater. Mama Love: worked in Taft High cafeteria on the boys who were only out to seed the girls. Saved a whole lot of lives.

Melody recites these and other facts when she comes out the empty house on Intervale. And then she usually has a man on her arm. She say all sorts of interesting things. She shows them how smart she is, book smart. They like the way her body tastes. They don't mind the book smarts that go along with her. Her mind is tremendous, like a brick building on its own. But I realize that that is only one way to love her.

One time she was a loud regular girl of the streets, but then she changed. Her niceness came with the dawn of her craziness. Suddenly she stood in the street and gave people directions. People our ways don't get lost a lot around here, why should they? But if someone gets to Longwood Avenue and they realize they are lost and they start to panic and pick fights to protect themself, Melody comes to them and calms them down. She tells them to go the way they came. Just look at the humps and cracks in the pavement and see if you remember them. That man standing in the doorway of that candy store smoking that clove cigarette. Those bottles on top of that open car where the rain has rained in the broken windows. That cat sleeping like a baby next to that hole near the curb. That big puddle in the sidewalk that looks like Africa. That golden-haired girl waiting on the corner with her bright new blue baby stroller. That table that somebody had put halfway out the second-floor window, that table simply hanging there.

Go on, remember. That will take you back to safety. Don't get mad. Don't go hitting somebody. You'll get back to safety. I will be your safety. You can trust me.

When I left my mother's the first time, she told me to take my lying ass out her home. Why did I want to go and mess her life like that? I told on my stepfather, that he had been coming into my room at night and first poking my titties with something, I don't know, and then one night, New Year's, he tried to set the nipples on fire with a lighter. And I was screaming, trying to pull away. Then he said no, I want to dip them in champagne and drink in a Happy New Year. One thing after the other. It looked unbroken.

So I used to watch this girl who started to live in the street, and I used to dream. She could dance, too, and she did it at all hours after she came from the empty house on Intervale. And some boys liked to look at her when she danced a storm. And from my window me usually thinking: I want any of you to look at me like that. But I don't say it. I stay where I am.

So my old mother comes to my place on Fox Street and it's been six years since I left hers, close to more. The first thing she says is: Your stepfather says you did it on purpose, but I don't want to think about those things, if you people insist on disbelieving that the Lord watches everything you do, then there ain't a damn thing I can say. And she pushes the vitamin bottles off the sill, she swoops them off as though they are dangerous and then looks at Melody dancing in the rain in the street. This day Melody is not alone. She is tying up the pack of dogs she found in the lot next to the empty house and she is combing their fur. From where I am, on the sixth floor, I can see she is giving them names. I can see her lips move. She says, Angela. Delilah. Betty. George. Frankie and Ishmael, husband and wife. They like the way her hands feel on their wet cold smelly dog bodies. It is a chill outside. Late winter laughable showers.

My mother says, That girl is the most fucked-up person I have ever seen. How can she do that to her family? Thirty years old and out her fucking mind. A job was what that stupid thing needed. No school. That woulda kept her mind clear.

I say, What do you know? You never worked a day in your life. Those Jehovah's Witnesses got you up there doing "secretary" work, but that ain't nothing. They just want you up there because you make it easy for them to steal everybody else's money.

She says, That girl's family must have no end in suffering. Being that their daughter is such a disgrace and all. And her poor mother especially. What a cross to bear.

I say back to her, Melody ain't hurting nobody. She is doing what makes her and a whole lot of other people happy. She knows about people's feelings.

My mother says, Don't give me that.

She looks at the vitamin bottles on the floor and holds the beta carotene up to the light, the one I had to go to Manhattan for, and she frowns. She has a new set of braids in and that's all she has been talking about, and it does make me happy in a way to see her mind on something good. She is proud of the way the gray blends in with the red and brown braids. She likes to look at the young girls strolling around the Hub and thinking their shit is so great, because then she can say to them: Takes one to know one. People laugh at her. The way she swings her head. Her big tight butt. She laughs back.

Mostly she thinks her extensions give her the old power she had when I was living with her and her husband and my baby Tee all under the same roof. I was a slave to the house at that time. Mopping dusting taking out the garbage ironing sitting on my stepfather's lap if I wanted to watch the music video program cooking vacuuming vacuuming. Now I am not a slave. And whatever he got, he got what he deserves.

My old moms says, You still taking these? And by that she means the vitamins and she also knows the answer to that. So I feel an attitude coming on in me. I really hate that shit. My moms is good at putting her head in the dirt. She should be called the ostrich woman. I'm thinking: You know why, old lady. Don't give me that.

But I can't get a word out my mouth before we both hear Melody scream outside. We get up and look out the window. Melody, my pretty girl, is shaking a dog's jaw off her hand. It won't let up. Moms laughs. She says, Idiot girl, no wonder her mother just gave up. And my mother, she shakes her head and laughs and kicks the vitamin bottles away from her feet. She says, I don't want to see any more of this garbage, these ain't the truth. And she tosses the beta carotene on my little bed. I had to travel with the 6 train all the way to Union Square for that. The discount store right across from the world-famous disco. I used to dance there when boys wanted me.

I call out the window, *Melody!* But my window is closed, painted shut at the trim. *Melody! Kick him! Scream louder! Kick him! Kick him! He'll leave you alone if you scream loud!*

Moms says, Come away from that window. What a cross

her poor mother has to bear. But that's what the good Lord gave her to eat off her plate.

I tell Moms, Shut up please! Melody ain't nobody's cross. But I know that's not true. She is my cross. I leave the apartment and flash down the stairs and see about her. When I get there, though, she is gone. The dogs are all in a row, like children in a school, licking each other's heads in the rain, but Melody is nowhere to be seen. And I feel my heart slice open. Sometimes I dream about getting her to live with me. I would like to go to bed with her in my arms at night. I would like to protect her.

When I get back, Moms doesn't wait. She throws the bowl at me that was also on the sill that was full of leftover medicine like nasal spray and stomach antacid. It hits me, makes my lip bloody.

I'm leaving, she says. She is swinging her extensions. I'm out the door. You seems to forget who you are talking to. You runs out of here for a lunatic. The Lord will visit you upon your sins. It's all out of my hands. Moms looks young. She doesn't let my Tee or Charlene call her "grandma."

She yells, And don't let me see none of this around here no more! She's pointing to the vitamin-bottle mess on the floor. The rug underneath the broken bottles was a present from Ty. He used to give me presents and things when he was around. He used to bother me too. I am sorry for his being gone. I miss his bothering me.

The vitamin bottles, they are thirty-two in all. They scare my moms. If I wasn't here, she would flush them all down the toilet. She doesn't like things that remind you of something horrible.

I want to calm her down, but now she is stamping on the bottles, looking like one of those big-bust, big-ass-in-a-tight-dress ladies down at the Kingdom Hall that suddenly got the spirit. Stamp. Stamp and flail. This is my young-looking mother here. Arms all flying around the room, head swerving with braid antennas that mark where she's going and where she's been. She picks up a few record albums on the bed and flings them like they are flying saucers. She tries to tear at the bedspread, but it's stronger than her. This makes her stop, think about who she's dealing with, and then bawl.

I am about to smack her one even though she is my mother because *shoot!* those vitamins cost me big-time and I don't have a hand helping me out anywhere. It's just only my hands. None of this shit comes free. And plus it costs money to go back and forth to Manhattan, and then there are the headaches. If it sounds like I am complaining, believe me.

I pull my mother away from the bedspread and make her sit on the bed. She breaks down crying even more, but what do you expect when this is a record that plays the same old song every time in a different tune? I can't scream at her like she rightfully deserves. One of her braids falls off. I pick it up and weave it back into her head.

She says, Why can't you put your faith in God? He can do it all for you.

My part of the record goes, Now don't you start up with all that shit again, Moms. God don't pay for vitamins. God don't stop my head from aching. God ain't going to attend my funeral.

Why you taking all these vitamins, she whimpers.

Just a precaution, I answer. Because in those days I was afraid of anything resembling the truth, too. I am my mother's daughter, when it all gets boiled down.

Which makes Moms cry more *again* and I am sorry for saying that (but it is my part of the record). She was there when I got back from the center. The time when they gave me a piece of paper saying: inconclusive. She was there in the room and just shook her head and said: All that nonsense, you going to be all right, see? And that's when she became a full-fledged Jehovah's Witness, not just a part-timer. You tell me.

So she is crying into the bedspread, and I am holding her from breaking and I'm thinking: Ain't this some shit? I hate you for taking your head out the sand every now and then. Do us both a favor. Go back to your old ways.

I glance out the window and there's Melody. She is smiling, and the rain has let up. But the sun is gone for good. And I'm thinking: If I'd a gotten a college education, I sure as hell wouldn't go crazy. I'd try really hard not to.

She has all the dogs lined up in a row and she is teaching them how to smile. The dog who was on her hand is lying on its side not moving. There is a brick next to him, and you can tell that the other dogs want to sniff him. That Melody.

She starts singing, "Don't Make Me Wait Another Day." And her smile is incredible. I can taste her lips from where I am watching. She puts her arms around the dogs' shoulders each and kisses their eyes.

I'm trying hard to comfort Moms. When I get up and come back with a cup of instant cocoa, she smacks it out my hand and makes me burn myself. She says, Look at you, girl! Your hair isn't combed! You as fat as a house! Lose that big behind! Get you a man back in your life so you don't wind up insane, learn to take care of yourself.

Damn, honey! Drinking this hot chocolate! You don't need to be drinking this! How are you going to get a man? How are you going to interest a man when the only thing on your mind is food? Ain't nobody going to want to love such a fat ass! Nobody save your old moms. But she can do only so much. And here you are looking a fright and staring out at some crazy girl in the street who tore her mother's heart to pieces. Shit.

That's the *real* reason you all alone, girl.

DECEMBER 7, 1991

The lady at the center said, Call me Mary. Let's be friends. No matter what, I don't want you to be afraid.

Don't worry, I said, I'm cool. I was cool. I wasn't going to let her think she knew more than me. I was wearing my leather miniskirt. I was letting her know that I still felt cool no matter what.

She said, Regardless of what anybody else says, you have to keep on keeping on. We all have days when clouds threaten. But you, I can tell you're super. You're a super-woman. It sounded like Mary had tears in her voice.

Before I left this morning, I told my mother who was sitting there in the kitchen with her McDonald's breakfast to make sure her husband didn't come by me again with his foolishness. She asked, What? I said, I stopped by to see you and he walked past me in the living room and did something to himself. And I'm not even living here anymore. What right does he think he has to do that? Moms said, Why do we live in such a ugly world, Lord help me.

So with this center lady, I am cool, I am totally together and shit. Ain't no big deal. Ain't nothing going to scare me to death. But I can feel my leg tapping against her desk.

She asks me how did I hear about their place. I tell her about Lorrie the friend I had who used to rave about them, how they helped men like him who loved men and were now afraid, men who were sick and were powerful afraid, and how good it was to be cared about, and don't you ever be afraid to go there if you need to. People there are kind to you, and they can hook you up if you need it. Lorrie couldn't believe there were such nice folks on the earth. He told me that this was really his home. And then he used to cry when he said it, and I used to think he was crying for joy for finding it, but when I asked him, he said no, he wasn't. Things like that shouldn't take a lifetime to find out.

Mary says, The regular counselor, Katie, is out sick today. The one you spoke to on the phone. That's why I am here. Do you understand me? Don't be afraid.

I'm not, I say. And I mean it. But I don't know why she is talking so loud and slow.

She explains to me a whole lot about the test. She keeps telling me to think on the positive side. No pun intended, get it? Her hair is blond and her voice is not from New York. Not from Manhattan, not from Brooklyn, especially not from the Bronx, where I have lived my whole life. She looks like she goes home at night and she can switch off the whole day behind her. She can take off her shoes and find a good place for them and make herself some tea and decide what she wants to eat and when and nobody can say anything against it. She can go to sleep at night without nobody bothering her in her sleep.

Mary says I should be glad I have friends who care enough to tell me about their place. At the center they are all like a family, there.

I say, My friend doesn't care anymore because he is dead. It comes out hard but I don't mean it in that way. Mary's face turns flabby and flat. Her eyes go downward, but they are wide open. Excuse me, she says, and gets up and leaves the room.

Then I get fidgety and get up out my seat and walk over to the wall and look at the posters there. One has three teenage girls playing around with each other at a slumber party. Their hair is all cute up in curlers. And I am reminiscing: Shit, I used to look like that. I used to be a teenager, a young one who used to have fun. I met Ty and he was my whole new world. Then the kids. You could say that the fun stopped when I hit the end of my teenage years at fourteen. In the poster, the girls are jolly, holding each other.

At the bottom it says, "Don't be a victim" and it's all about this one girl (I guess now a full-grown lady) talking about all the fun times these three girls used to have as kids, playing, dreaming about getting boys and other kinds of success. That was as kids. Now one of them has AIDS. Now normally most people would turn their back on her but not these two friends. They love their friend now more than ever. In their mind, they will always be the Three Love Diviners. That's what they called themselves when they were dreaming of a singing career. At the bottom of the poster it says "Together We Can Fight AIDS." Love Diviners.

Mary comes back into the room with a little cup of water and says, Tell me about your children. She drinks the water and studies me.

I return to my seat in her small office with no window and tell her about Tee and how he is now seven years old and damn near smarter than his teacher. Sometimes he gets hit for being so smart but that's okay. He has to learn.

I love me some Tee. Named after his father who at first didn't want to see him. But then the father jones started kicking in. Ty bought me a stroller from Wowow's as a baby shower gift. He didn't give it to me in person, though. He called me from the bodega on Prospect Avenue to tell me to look out my front door. Then he hung up. So I walked down eight floors and I find the stroller. My mother who was there for the shower said, "Oh he really does care, see? You are in some deep shit." The next day Ty called me from the bus station in Washington D.C. to see how I liked it. He said he was glad I liked it. And that he would call me when he got back to the Bronx. Take care of yourself.

I tell Mary about Charlene. She is still a baby by all rights.

Gets into every damn thing. I'm not really sure I love her. I tell Mary that I always remember to feed her, but sometimes it's like I forget she is lying there, waiting for me.

Mary offers me a dried sugar fig from her desk drawer. Then she tells me how brave I am being and all kinds of shit. She asks me do I feel like crying, because I can do it right there if I feel like it. She is here to care. I just look at her. Then she jumps up and runs out the office. I hear her talking to her boss, another white lady with blond hair. Only she looks like she is from the Bronx.

And my mind has to go back to this poster behind me. I think that the only thing it doesn't say is how the girl's friends feel once they found out how she got AIDS. Did she fuck a boy she didn't hardly know? Did somebody tell her it was her own damn fault then? Did she shoot up with some respectable-looking people who worked for a downtown company in Manhattan? Did she cry to her family first and then to her two friends? Did one of them say to her at first, There's no other word for you but *ho!* Did she have to first die like that?

The white boss lady comes in and says, Miss Jackson, please forgive Mary's unprofessional behavior. She's new around here. Would you rather talk to me?

In a minute the boss says, Miss Jackson, your results are inconclusive. That means, in short, that you will have to come back and take another test. Understand? It doesn't mean positive or negative. It means: come back.

Okay, I say. She begins to tell me the details, on and on. My head is slivering on the inside. Mary comes back into the room and puts her hand on my shoulder. Then she says in my direction, You are a superwoman, I really admire you so much, I do. Then they both leave.

Me, I look in the mirror next to the poster and I make sure that my hair is in place. I just permed it this morning. Curls frame my angel face. And I feel in my pocket for a subway token that will take me back to the Bronx. I hate coming to Manhattan. Nobody cares here. Everyone is rushing and even when they do stop to see what's going on, you are about as noticeable as a sidewalk or a building.

My hair is okay. I put on Forbidden lipstick. I'm wearing the miniskirt Ty bought me for my birthday last year. Hey, I look good. I am cool. Can't nobody tell me anything else. I stand up and look in the mirror at my whole body. I lift a little cup of water that Mary has on her desk and I bring it to my lips. It looks great. It all looks great. I stay in there for about half an hour, in her chair. I am not just super. I am *supernatural.*

DECEMBER 3, 1990

I hear her voice smearing itself all over me, like coffee-flavored jam. Get it? Jam's not supposed to taste like coffee, have you ever heard of such a nasty thing?

Misshoneysugarbaby. Missyhoneybabysugarsugar. Missything. Where do you think you're going? And why ain't you said hi? *Misshoney?* Am I invisible? And why you start walking faster every time you see me? Tell me! Don't be turning your head like you don't care when I talk to you! I got me something important to say! *Babygirldarlinsugar:* I'm having me a party, and it's going to be the deffest jam of all time, shit, it's really going to be smokin! Bring your girl ass on over! I'm going to have the finest-rate boys over there, you know, the ones that be just like chocolates, dark ones plain, dark ones with a nut inside, brown ones with cream in the middle, yellow ones with a cherry! And you know I be after the ones with a cherry! *Sugarsugar* please come. Please come. You and me ain't had the chance to be friends, seems like after all these years you been sitting up here in my neighborhood but you don't really see me, you don't want to notice me anymore, I always dream of us being friends, no, of us being sisters. You know, we so much alike. You and I, we the same thing when you get down to it. *Honeysweetthing?* Answer me! Answer me.

I just look at this chick. I know I ain't seen her since our high school days, but shit. Here we are, old people practically. Ain't that when you have been supposed to have learned something about the world? Shit.

Her name is Laura Washington only 'cause Skeeter Washington married her for a baby. Back in the days it was just Laura. Or Laura the white girl. Or Laura the white girl we all hate. Get on back to the Italian section where you run from. She had Skeeter's baby. He had wanted white pussy. So she went ahead and volunteered herself and then she was surprised to see what happened next: a bunch of folks in the neighborhood just laughing their head off at her. Or the old ones just shaking their head at her in the stores on Third Avenue. Or the Dominican ones who tried to say a prayer for her behind her back on the street, then cursed her out. My mother's house was miserable at the time for me, but I would never have traded places with the white girl who wanted to be black. Not for all the coffee in China.

Laura ran around showing her baby off and grinning like it was her passport, like now she would belong no matter what. Some old church ladies would pick the baby up out its stroller and say, Ain't you a pretty thing? Being a white girl's baby and all. You sure is a pretty thing.

Laura didn't like that none. She would be showing off her baby and try to hook it together with her man, so she would have more tightness with folks. Skeeter would be walking around the street, and she would stop and yell out something at him and he would slowly turn his face her way and say something like, Yes, I will buy you formula. Yes, I'ma give you twenty bucks, so shut up. No, I don't know when I'm coming in tonight. Don't be on my case, stupid. Don't ask me what's on my mind.

Girls on their way to Jane Addams would cut their eyes at her and say: You think your shit is that good? Well, his dick ain't starving *that* much! He'll be back.

Laura brought the baby out even when it snowed. I used to say hi to her, that's all. She made my heart move in her pitiful way. But then I stopped. My moms saw me talking to Laura and said, You know that girl be out there tricking? Why don't she just move back to the Italian section with her folks? Tricking ain't gonna make her more of us. There *are* some of us that do have a regular job.

Because one day soon after that I was out walking Tee and it was when my stomach was beginning to grumble in the usual baby way, and I was thinking Shit, is this for real? and there in front of me was Laura coming out the boarded building on Intervale pushing her baby stroller and tugging at my stepfather's arm, who was following after her. She started arguing with him. He pulled out his pants pockets to show they were empty. And he was grinning, not looking sad or worried. Then Laura started cursing him out so much that her face turned red as her hair and her hands started automatically shaking the stroller. I had to think about the time Ty said he was going to get me an apartment for me and the baby and then next thing I knew, he was at his aunt's house in Washington D.C. It didn't matter how much I cried. His Aunt Deborah got on the phone herself and told me to leave them alone, couldn't I just let him get on with his life?

So there was Laura up there arguing with my stepfather and like magic, a cop car comes out of nowhere and asks them what the problem is. And my stepfather is talking and Laura slowly puts her face in her hands. Her shoulders go up and down. The baby starts wailing. People look them up and down and keep on moving along the sidewalk. Skeeter is sitting on top of a car two blocks away on Fox Street, observing. The cop puts his hand on Laura's shoulder and she gets all hysterical and shit, like she is going to belt this man one. The cop is getting angry, but before he can do anything, Laura turns around and spits on him and picks up the baby stroller and starts wheeling it down the street. The cop yells, Get in the car, miss. But Laura keeps moving.

Then him and my stepfather converse a little bit. The cop leaves. My stepfather walks in my direction.

Laura is stomping down the sidewalk. Some boys see her and follow her and scream, There you have it!

Laura's hair was red. It used to be brown, blond once. She was still skinny, just like in high school. She looked like a little girl wheeling her baby doll in a toy carriage. Her face was small. Her arms and legs were small. The way she walked that day, I was wondering if she remembered her mother, and if someone ever looked in her face and said, You *have* something.

Now she looks at me like I am the answer. Laura says to me, Girl, I been thinking bout you, missing you. Remember how you always used to say hi to me? You never forgot to say hi. I wish we could hook up again. You and me, we alike.

Nah, I tell her. We aren't like. I'm not your sister. There's none of me in you. I saw you with my stepfather. If you *think* you made me sick, you only know the half of it.

Oh yes there is you in me, Laura says, smiling. I want to feel sorry for her, but I force myself not to. I want to love her just a touch. But I can't. I know what she is saying is true. I don't know how she knows it, but it's true. And that makes me hate myself, like a trash heap.

She says to me in a soft voice, Honey.

Then Laura turns around and gets on a nauseous face. She's wearing a blue jeans jacket with red and black sequins on it. On the back they spell *Missy Miss.* She got herself a rap name. Now she's vomiting up brown, and she falls to her knees. I look at her. She looks like a prayer. Folks pass and don't bother to stare.

She finishes and looks up at me and says, You and me, Lay, *girlhoneysugarbabysugar,* we a lot alike. There's no getting away from that fact.

AUGUST 20, 1989

I hate coming to Lorrie's grave. He's been dead for a couple a months but his mother is always here, every day, like it was yesterday. And that makes me angry. Shit, can't anybody have a place for their sad? Why does she have to crowd everybody out? Lorrie probably feels squeezed out his grave by now.

I see her up here today. It's raining, cold as hell, dark like the cemeteries in the horror flicks. But she is not wearing any coat, only a dress and grandmother black pointy-toe shoes. She doesn't even have stockings on. Something about her reminds me of Aunt Jemima, with her church-lady bra *out to here,* but I guess she can't help it. Today like the other days she is kneeling and her dress has mud all over the bottom. She has her hands clasped. Sometimes she makes me so fucking aggravated with her long sorrow.

She notices me and waves me down. She used to hate me but now all she has the strength for is to reminisce about her gone son. So she thinks I am going to stand here in the rain and talk all those old memories of Lorrie. All I want to do is see his grave and go home. Every time I come out here to Astoria it pours. But Lorrie's mother wants to talk and re-member. She acts like it has been years and not just months that Lorrie is buried. She has to keep up the talk so he won't disappear into the ground with the worms and the little pebbles.

Today she doesn't even say hi. She's already in full swing.

She shouts, You know, he was one of the few victims who got a real burial. No cremation for my boy. No sir. Lorrie was going out with dignity. A real burial with a real funeral and a real casket. A real reverend.

I say, You already done told me that, Mrs. Adams. I was there, don't you remember?

She says, Girl, you *weren't* there when the doctors tried to get me to burn my baby's body! Honey, you ain't heard their words! They told me the worst fucking crap.

I'm not used to Mrs. Adams cursing. She is a mother of the Church of God in Christ on Prospect.

I say, Yes ma'am, I done heard it all already.

She says, Telling me all this bullshit. Like nobody with that illness should get buried, only cremated cause who knows if some of that AIDS won't creep out the ground and contaminate. What do I look like, girl? I ain't no fool. My boy ain't going to contaminate. Alls he's gonna do is lie there. And wait for me. God will allow us to reunite at the Appointed Hour.

I say, I know that, Mrs. Adams. Where's your coat, it's cold out here, let's not go rushing you to the grave. I say this because I am not a total monster when it comes to Lorrie's mother.

She shouts again, But I told them, honey, *you got to believe me when I say I told them!* If you don't let me bury this boy's body, you will have to bury mine. Cause I'm gonna die trying. Cause this my baby here. Not no firelog.

And I am thinking: Shut up, lady. And don't even try to run away from it: he was dead before he died. You see, he liked being fucked in the butt. Only he couldn't tell you nothing about that. You wanted him to love your neighbor's daughter, Zenzile Jones. Oh no, you couldn't see.

But I say, Mrs. Adams, no one is going to forget Lorrie anytime soon. But he does need to have some peace in the grave. We need to do more than just survive.

And I get up to leave. She doesn't turn to me. She tries to adjust her knees, but the mud has her stuck there, in that one position, looking like a dizzy angel, with her son.

JUNE 22, 1989

I don't feel well. When I look in the mirror, all I see is a gray girl. My eyes look gray, my face is the same color as old newspaper. My ears burn all the time. Yesterday I was so nervous I couldn't stop going to the bathroom. What is wrong with the machine? I am not pregnant. Charlene is the last one for me. People don't realize how hard it is to have a baby, to go through all those months eating and feeling like a pig, sleeping on the subway even if you only got two or three stops to make, looking for big clothes to wear because the maternity stuff is crazy expensive. And it is also hard when no one else has you in their evening of universe or needs to hear your voice say their name.

I'm always tired these days. Yesterday my legs felt so lumbery that I couldn't hardly walk nowhere. Whenever I opened my mouth, the breath inside made my moms frown and say, Girl, you could wake the living dead.

Moms was by my new place on Longwood Avenue. I left Zenzile Jones's family's apartment and got this place all on my own. It's one room on Longwood, over the Salvation Army store, but it's mines. The kids have a space near my bed. It's enough for us because we are enough for us. We are a family in here.

Moms put her hand on my forehead. I liked the way it felt

there. But I can't say that that was a memory from childhood. When I was coming up with Moms, it was every man for himself. Now she told me to lie down. I liked the way that sounded coming over her lips.

We used to look so much alike, Moms and me. Both of us had the same hair, Chinese eyes, mouth shaped like an upside-down U, crinkly forehead getting all lined even when we were happy. Moms's hair is turning gray, and so is mine, only I am still in my greenery, so she says.

So she said, I don't like the way you look. All run down. What's the matter, baby?

And I don't have to tell you how long it's been since Moms has called me her baby. The world is capable of frightening, welcome things.

I told her how I felt. She put me to bed and gave me some aspirin. She ran her eyes over my room. Table, lamp, sofa bed with me in it, sky-blue wallpaper, kitchen sink and cabinet, refrigerator holding beer and eggs and baby food and hot-dog rolls, a stack of books on the floor and a TV on top of them. Moms asked, You got a Bible anywhere? I tell her no, and I feel anger coming on, but I keep myself cool. Moms picks up Tee's book of Mother Goose and reads out loud the rhyme about the mother in the shoe. Then she reaches over and kisses my head. Then she rocks me to sleep.

When I wake up, it is dark outside and the summer rain has started. Moms has got rice and greens on the stove and a pork chop and is pouring me out a glass of milk. She says to me, This is how you need to eat from now on. No more beer. You could hurt another life like that. Here, eat this. Tomorrow I am going to get you some vitamins.

DECEMBER 7, 1988
Ty loves his boy. He wants to throw him a four-year-old birthday party — at the Winning Gentleman's Club over on

53rd Street in Manhattan. Shit, is he crazy? They wouldn't allow me in there. Ty just wants one of the dancers there to look at him.

He likes to hold Tee in his lap on the chair by the stove. He likes to read Mother Goose out loud. He visits us a whole lot, every other day or so. This would be our family home if Ty could get his shit together. *The reason he doesn't?* He says he falls in and out of love with me. And maybe that means two people don't deserve each other that much. When he starts in with all that, all I can say is: *Don't you hear me talking to you, baby?* and I remind him of how I've been there for him, always. I don't have to tell him twice.

At night Ty's hands are on my titties. I'm lucky to have such big ones, they do work to improve the way people notice you. 40 D. We are all in one room, next door to his Aunt Nettie's apartment who knows when and where her nephew's hands are. She has x-ray ears that can decipher through cement walls. When Ty starts pursuing my titties and his hands are on me like spiderwebs, Nettie calls out from her apartment next door, This building doesn't just belong to you all! She makes us laugh, but there is something spooky about it that leaves us having sex louder and louder.

In his sleep, Ty calls out my name. Or sometimes he cries out "Sweet potato pie" or "Dance, dance, dance" in his sleep. When he wakes me up, it is all I can do not to squeeze him to death in love.

MARCH 3, 1988
There's this girl in the street I watch over and over. Some people say she is crazy. She wears her nightgown in the street in broad daylight and it does look crazy. She calls out somebody's name, picks up garbage, conversates with people walking by and also with parked cars, puts her face up to

store windows, and once I even seen her dip her face in a puddle.

When the kids line up to get a ice cream cone (even though it is cold outside), this crazy girl goes up to the front of the line and says to the ice cream man, What about mine? So he gives her something, something little, a candy. Then she will stare hard at him and say, Don't pretend you don't see me here. *I am all over this place!* She doesn't like it that she has only got something little. The kids all get their Popsicles and laugh at her. They think, The girl is bugging, the girl is missing a few screws. And she joins in the laughing cause she don't know night from day.

JULY 4, 1987

This block, I never really thought about it too much. Brook Ave. It's never been my home and it's always been my home. I like the four or five trees. I like that some of us know all the potholes, all the tire skids and craters in the sidewalk, the store windows full of rice. A sexy girl in a beer ad on the side of an apartment, letting the frost melt between her softness. It's a hot day, and everyone I know is out. I'm looking at all of them from my bedroom window, leaning out, the air is thick and unbreatheable and there is a faithful haze over every damn thing. I notice the fire escapes, the bricks, the sewer grates with folded candy wrappers in them. It's my street. Sometimes it's my home, and sometimes it's not. I snuggle in my blankets in the blazing July sun and let the sweat rock me to sleep.

can you say
my name?

WE HAVE TWO facts in front of us. One: babies, once they're here, stay, and can do our work for us; and two: men love love. Bri threw up in homeroom almost every day and it seemed like a awful commotion. But whenever she turned around and saw Roc two rows back and felt his blue eyes reciprocating love and understanding, it was like it was *his* hands that were wiping up her mouth, all the baby throw-up, and not the teacher's, Mr. Hancock's, who was scared shitless, and so Bri didn't have anything to fear. Me, I'm still waiting. I'm trying to reciprocate, but I'm doing it alone. Boy Commerce bops past me in the hall on his way to practice and sometimes has a stone frown, or sometimes he laughs all in my face when he catches me rubbing my belly. He don't talk to me anymore. He pretends to dis me any chance he gets. Like when he knows I'm following him down the hall, he'll put his hand up some other girl's ass and say, "Did I do that? Sorry," like it's supposed to really make the girl laugh, like I'm supposed to get jealous and shit.

He pretends to dis me. But it ain't no real disrespect, cause it's strange, but you know deep in your heart that one day your waiting will come to an end. My plan is gold. I can even go so far as to say this: that whenever I look at Boy Commerce, I see him as the black ship sailing out to the wide free sea, and me as one of the slaves in the hold. Like we learn about in school and are supposed to feel proud of. The waves are crashing against the side of the boat and the dolphins are trying to catch the sun rays in their open mouths with their tiny rows of teeth and I am licking the toes of the other slaves lying around me. Maybe there is something else out there, but I am the one who dies in the hold, on the trip to the New World, the new life. I will never leave. I will stay on the ship. There is not a damn thing to fear.

Do you like tongue kissing a dog? No, I ain't tried that shit. *Would you try it for me?* Hell, are you crazy? *No, I ain't, it's real simple, all you do is pretend you got someone in your arms that is ready for you to do just about anything, and you're hot tonight.* Shit, that's some sick shit, I will never put my mouth on a dog's. *Then you won't ever put your mouth on mine.* Don't say that. *I just did.* Why you treat me like this, don't you know my loving is all for you, you my number one, ain't nothing gonna come between us? *Look, I'm not asking for too much, just something little and crazy, you want to prove you will do anything I say, that's what I call love!* But that dog been licking his ass. *The dog's mouth is clean, and I just want to see you do it, please baby.* I only want your kisses. *I just want to see.* Will you promise to never leave me, I'm doing this crazy shit only for you and you better not fucking go nowhere. *I just want to see.* Look, I'm the boss now, and I want you to promise you will never leave, because you can't imagine how much I love you. Please. *Please.* Please.

Bri and me decided in ninth grade that we were going to be wives in school. The homegirl cheerleaders turned up their noses and shook their asses at us. One of them, Sam, said to me, "You got to lose that shit, girl! There *are* other ways to get out, and the one you doing is crack open for a dick and get a public assistance check shoved up there instead. Don't get it too wet or they won't cash it." Vulgar. Another one, Mandy with the imported African box braids, said, "Become a cheerleader! This way you can save yourself all by yourself, and *then* the shit that the adoring homeboys serve up to you is choice!" Teeny, cornrow cheerleader, said, "Geez Christ, mens do pain us!" The last time any one of them said anything, it was Marge, real name Margarita Floretta Inez Santamaria, who really could've had any boy in the whole damn school: "You will go through all that work but you ain't gonna have the reward. You gonna be two women sitting alone in the laundromat, dreaming about humping a tube of toothpaste when you get home."

Me and Bri laughed them off. *Yo yo:* we are homegirls and you know we know the deal better than anyone else and their mama and their mama's mama.

The teachers didn't think we were so crazy. One of them, the old science lady, puckered up: You folks are all the same. Laying up under men like that. It's a God-honest shame. Don't you ever wonder where you'll be?

Mrs. Mary, the Irish teacher who used to be in Catholic school, chimed in: No, they sure as hell don't. We show them the history of the world, and they are doomed to repeat all the mistakes. They just want to spend the rest of their born days right here!

Mrs. Faulkner, Elizabeth Taylor lookalike, sewing homeroom: Here? But they'll just wind up statistics! Heavens! Don't you think we should perhaps guide them . . . at least a little into the light?

Blond sissy-ass Mr. Hancock, math teacher and homeroom: You mean *our* way! Are you kidding, Althea? We don't want them our way! Let them stay the fuck where they are. They ain't got a clue. And I ain't gonna be the one to give it to them.

(*Wrong*, of course, because that dumb fake-English-accent ass was the one who didn't have the clue! We had the clues, we were on the money. Somehow. Still, all this talk tended to make Bri get all nervy, and she would start asking, "Toya, do we know what we're actually gone do? I mean, should we have babies or become junior-year cheerleaders?" Bri was always the unsteady one. I started to get sick of that shit, but then again: I didn't want to do it all alone. So I calmed her down, because she couldn't figure a damn thing out. The only thing she seemed to get together was this Africa thing. Wearing the African-looking clothes, gold bamboo earrings, a map of Africa on her jacket. She was really into that before-slavery shit. She called me her sister under the skin. She even wanted us to give each other African names, like Tashima and Chaka, Myesha, Zenzile, Aminata, and things. Like that is going to solve some shit! Sometimes she made me sicker than the baby throw-up.)

Bri was always freaking about the baby, but I managed to talk her out of her commotion and even got her to make a compromise: she relaxed her hair like the cheerleaders but wore T-shirts that said B A B Y = 1+1 and S O M E B O D Y D O W N T H E R E L O V E S M E .

There was no question for me. I was going to be a wife in school. Boy Commerce was planning on a basketball scholarship so I'd have me an educated man. I *do* have a clue. It's just that people have clouded-up, fucked-up minds, and they refuse to see the truth and they live like snails underground in a garden, slimy. Blind. Dark. Like that hold.

Why you being so good to me all of a sudden, I thought you was mad at me, baby. Me, hell no, I just think I'm finally ready to give you all my loving. What's that supposed to mean, what I ain't already got? Me, the whole me, my heart. Well then, hurry up and give it. It's yours for the taking. *I like that shit, lemme feel your lovin.*

My Uncle Marion busted his best pair of glasses upside my head. "You what?" He rammed me into the refrigerator, so hard the door popped open and the milk crashed on the floor. *Big-time dis!* "Ho, ho, you been ho'ing in my house!" He had the wooden spoon, the one that used to belong to my mother and me on Delancey Street, and he was drumming out a funeral march on my ears. (I admit, it was hard not to bust out crying, but I kept my plan in mind, and that was like my light at the end of the tunnel.) "Ho! You get what you deserve! Grinding up neath that boy! You worse than a African! Is that how I raised you? Is that how I done?" Uncle Marion grabbed one of my cheeks and tugged till his nails left his permanent mark of love on me. "Ho! What was you thinking?"

Don't say nothing till it's too late to have an abortion.

It took a lot out of me to try and learn this scared-ass Bri the basics. I told her to keep on going to gym class, keep on doing the fifty warm-up pushups, hundred situps. Volunteer to be the kickball team captain, not just a regular player! Keep on wearing Wah Wah lipstick and doing your hair up like if someone better came along, you'd go for him and leave that other sorry ass — the one who was going to be your husband — behind. Don't put your head down on the desk because you say you're tired, or other kinds of baby-related shit. Be like you were in the old days and get the right answers and say them in front of the rest of the class: *you are still a genius like before.* Just don't zip up your pants, just wear a big sweater over so nobody sees you can't bend over no more. The gold plan. That's how you become a wife in time for Homecoming and Thanksgiving break.

I have been in love since the seventh grade. One day I sat in Reading with my large-print version of *Tale of Two Cities* propped up on my lap and dreamed of what I am doing now: being big with somebody's love. My destiny was as clear to me then as it is now. You might say that since I was a child then, I was illing because I was thinking I would be Boy Commerce's wife in tenth grade. But not so. You're only illing when you dream of things that can't possibly come true.

Bri took it upon herself to fall in love with Roc, and at first the cheerleaders said they wouldn't even consider looking at me or Bri because of this move of hers. Sam said that Bri was taking some white girl's boy away, and they didn't go for that, man-snatching, the cheerleaders. The only way the girls could be sure you wasn't playing dirty was if you had some homeboy or some Puerto Rican dude as yours. But I ask you: what do a white boy want with one of us for? What do Roc want with Bri, who's dark and not the prettiest girl you ever seen? That's some fucked-up shit. In my opinion, men like that only see the girl as a dark-skinned beauty, like some Pam Grier in the action movies, and they want to experience some bad pussy. Bri ought to have known that shit. And if it ain't that, then some white girl is crying her eyes out because her boy has left her for some dark ass. And that ain't right, because it's the same thing as man-stealing, and that goes against all cheerleader rules of order. We *are* all sisters when you get down to it.

Bri said love never happened like it was planned. She said love was a flower with no name in the garden of mankind. A flower like the kind that grew in the Motherland, *Africa*. She said, "You all are *illing*. This man wants me for me!" So she said she was going to prove it. Roc followed her around like a puppy. Once I caught them in the science lab, and it was like Roc's hands was straightening Bri's whole body like a relaxing comb. Smooth, broken, knotting-out movements. I laughed out loud. Bri flushed and was ashamed, and Roc said, "You can't stop me!" He looked scared like a true skinny white boy, but he did put his arms around big Bri to try and cover her up. I think that was the real reason Bri said she was going to be with Roc as his wife in school. Maybe if I hadn't a caught them planting the seed, maybe she would have left him afterwards. I had wanted to apologize, but they ran off dragging their clothes down the hall.

Bri was ashamed, and so I made it my job to convince her to stay with him because first: I knew she would never get a man like him (who loved love) again in this world, and two: I didn't want to be alone.

You know, I feel like I want to open up to you, ain't that weird? *Why? I feel the same way.* Nah, really, I'm not used to that kind of shit, and now I'm feeling like: hey, I want this girl to know a part of the real me. *I'm all ears, forever.* You know my father, he ain't raised me to be a sissy, he raised me to be a real man, and so it's hard, it's hard. *You want to lay your head on my shoulder?* I got things to do, I got places to see — but don't talk to me about any of that when I'm lying next to you making some good love. *What do you mean, places to go?* Baby, I got feelings, sometimes I just look at all the people in the street lying around, or sometimes I see my father dealing out a deck of cards and kissing my mother's cheek, and I start feeling so low. *Don't worry, you always got me.* Do you know I feel like killing my fucking self, getting on the track and touching the third rail? *Baby, don't say that shit, don't!* Word. *Don't.* That's how it gets to me sometimes, and I wonder: am I going to get a chance to kill myself, or will I just be buried alive? *BUT WHERE YOU TALKING ABOUT GOING, AM I GONNA BE WITH YOU, HOW DO I FIT IN BABY?* There you go talking all that shit, you don't listen to a word I say, do you? *Sure I do, baby, it's just I don't know where you thinking about going, that's all, and I always want to be there with you, understand?* I ain't talking about you, I'm talking about staying the fuck alive! *Don't worry, baby, with me, you will always be alive to the one who matters, now go on.*

I used to be five-foot-six with pretty box braids, skin the same color as the singer in that movie *Mahogany* and a nice voice. I could sing me some beautiful songs, like "Reveal Him to My Soul" and "Precious Is the Son." I used to be skinny and used to could dance to music. I used to go to parties with my mother's, then with Uncle Marion's permission. My nose came out in a perfect point, and I used to have dimples. Cute, you could've called me, or even a fox.

Then there is this time where everything disappears, everything. I make up my mind, I look in the mirror and make up my mind. Tired of all this being alone and shit. They all think they can book whenever they like.

Therefore, now I am five-foot-three with relaxed hair in a runt ponytail. I travel with a belly now. My face is spread out like a ocean, with rocks and seaweed in every wave. I always have throw-up in my mouth, sometimes I carry a little cup with me in the train. I don't dance at parties to the record player no more. I dance underneath a boy who says, "Put your butt this way, I am almost *there*."

I look into the mirror and still see a fox. Hell, I will go so far as to say: I am badder than bad.

I took Bri to the new Stop-One Supermarket and to Tiny-town's. She had to learn the good sides that were to come.

This was part of the gold plan. It's like we learned about in school: this was a science.

Look, I'ma show you what you don't learn in Home Economics. This here is the most important aisle: Borax, Mr. Clean, 2000 Flushes, Fantastic. You got to know how to keep your man happy, and this is gold. This is the surefire way. This is the way so that when his boys come over to check out the crib and hang and smoke some herb, you earn a A+.

This aisle is the lifesaving ring to the new wife and mother: Alpo, KittyKat Delight, Friskies, Yum Pup. Now, you can bet your bottom dollar that once you're in, the husband is going to want to get you a pet so you have some hobby to take your mind off the kid sometimes, because you don't want to go having a nervous breakdown on me, right? If it's a cat, then you also got to think about kitty litter, and somehow boys don't like cats too much, all that rubbing up on you and shit. Boys get jealous when they see the cat laying up with you in the bed and then they act like: it's them or me, and you about ready to fall out laughing because they sure as hell don't seem like grown husbands but like spoiled kids. But you don't laugh, you take the cat to a shelter. Let em get you a dog. Boys like to be around dogs because it makes them into men faster. It's the kind of thing where they can go out on a Sunday morning to the park and jog and run and play catch and think in the back of their minds: Hey, this shit is *down*, I'm feeling good. Husbands need to feel good. And that's when they thank their lucky stars they got us back at home. Dogs' breath sure do smell like shit, but just think of him in the park. You take the dog out for a walk in the weekday morning and let it protect the baby.

Here's my favorite aisle, because it always changes: diet foods and ethnic. They got all these Slim Control foods, like Slim Control Salad Dressing, Slim Control Apple Snack'ems, Slim Control Malted Milkshake. Slim Control is what's going to keep us going, girl! And they keep on getting more: Slim Control Ketchup, Slim Control Jelly. You can eat all this shit, then take one or two of their Slim Control Diet Pills and you aren't hungry for three days. Get it? You lose weight that's really not weight at all. And you can laugh at the men getting their beer bellies in front of the TV, because you ain't going to be in the same boat. Then the homies that come by the crib start checking you out. Wouldn't you love to stay skinny forever? Not blow up the way all those mothers do? We got to hold on to our world, honey, and this is the way we going to do it. I want Boy to fucking love me forever. I love Slim Control Cheddar Cheese Popcorn.

Bri, like I had figured, loved Tinytown's. She kept saying, "Oooh, I'ma get me this for the baby, oooh, I like this toy machine gun if it's a boy." Bri held the black baby dolls like they were her own and kissed their cheeks. She said they looked like African goddesses! I was thinking, This store is too goddamn expensive. My child will do like me in the old days: play in the bathtub with the spatula, the wooden spoon, the rice pot, the strainer. Man, I had me some good times once.

Bri asked the Tinytown saleslady how much the black baby doll was that said, "Can you say my name?" The saleslady said eighty-nine fifty. And do you believe Bri was thinking about asking her mother for the money for that thing? *Typical.* Ugly-ass doll. *Can you say my name!* But at least I got Bri to look for a moment at the positive side of motherhood and being a wife in school. I told Margarita Santamaria in the school cafeteria, Yeah we know what the hell we are doing.

Listen up I'm only gonna say this once I know I done some fucked-up things in life but it's never too late to make things change for the better, *you ain't done anything that fucked up*

*and listen we got more important things to talk about like
what's gonna be the name and when you coming over to
spend the night with me again,* shit Toya you ain't gonna let
me get a word in is you, *sorry,* sorry my ass, sorry.

Listen up we can still be together but don't you want to go
to college like me or you was talking about that business
school where you could learn something useful, *man all that
stuff's in the future we got other things to think about,* no
THIS IS WHAT WE NEED TO THINK ABOUT, *no this is
what we need to think about: are you always gonna be there
for me in other words are you always gonna be faithful?*

I want you to be happy even if I been doing some fucked-
up shit, *you mean with them other girls,* yeah I mean like
that, *shoot I know you don't really care about them,* yeah you
right I don't, *so why you bring them up?*

Because I want the chance to care about them, baby.

*Listen up you: I ain't going to college or business school or
nothing, when it comes you are gonna give it a name or else!*

Else what?

*Don't do like that because I know that what you really
want deep inside is love love love and that's what I got to give
let me show you again.*

Listen to me, LISTEN TO ME, listen to me, listen to me.

In seventh grade, my mother was still alive. The house on
Delancey Street was cold indoors because the bricks were
falling off outdoors. When I came home from school, I used
to have to feed her applesauce and overcooked vegetables
from a spoon. Uncle Marion called from his house on the
other side of the city, Washington Heights. He used to check
on us and ask how my mother's breasts were doing. I used to
have to hold Mother's head in my arms like a warm ball and
smooth out her hair with my hands, she couldn't take no

brush. She would ask me to sing "Unforgettable You" and "Breakaway" to her so she could sleep better. My voice was high in those days. I was in the after-school gospel singers. I used to love to sing, but only songs like "In Times Like These" and "Send a Message" — songs that gave you a good feeling, like you *are* in seventh grade and your whole life *is* spread out in front of you like a red carpet, but I hated it when her head dozed off in my arms. It made me too ancient.

Her favorite animals were fishes. She dug them all, angelfish, blue whales, sharks, dolphins. She liked the free way they swam the ocean. They moved without seams, without giving a thought to where their next breath was going to come from. They traveled light and always in a direction. They never dreamed about getting caught, about being on a dinner plate, about swimming in a tank before hundreds of hungry eyes. They let the currents brush them along, and they tasted ocean water the way we tasted the air in the room with the air conditioner on. Mother had the kind of wishing talking that cut deep when she spoke and when I held her head in my arms.

It was going okay, I thought. I did take good care of her. But then one day, sure as shit, Mother announced like she was a loudspeaker in a subway station, I am going to kill myself. She said, I won't be here for you when I do that, but you will have Uncle Marion. You can hold on to him.

I said, under the water of tears, "Don't you think you could change your mind? Don't you think you could think again and decide to stay with me till I am a grown-up? I want to hold on to you."

She said, You just don't understand the pain, Toya. It has to give way. I have to make it give way.

So she sent me off to Uncle Marion's house and she

drowned herself in poison air with her head laying in the gas oven. Uncle Marion said that was because her breasts were on fire on the inside, that's how he explained that shit to me then.

She couldn't stay for me. Damn, she couldn't even do it in the water, take her life where I knew she'd like to do it the most.

Mandy with the imported box braids said, "You *gots* to be crazy, baby! I ain't giving up being a cheerleader for nothing! And I don't want to have stretched-out legs!" Mandy had seven brothers and sisters and you could understand that she needed to spend all that time at cheerleader practice to get the hell away from them.

Margarita Santamaria said, "Bri, you aren't stupid. Do like I did."

Sam, head cheerleader, told us, "Naw, I see things different now. You girls is *on!* Lemme be the godmother, okay? I can give it a godname, right?"

Boy Commerce got cheerleader Sam's boyfriend, Big Daddy Dave, to let us into the biology lab. He had some big secret for me, Boy, he even held my hand on the way there from the boys' locker room. Big Daddy unlocked the door, and Boy held it open as I walked on through. He was like a real gentleman when he said to Big Daddy, "Catch you in a sec, bro."

I made sure to keep my hands off my belly. I didn't complain one time about my big swelled-up feet. I wore my old raincoat so Boy wouldn't have to notice my shape if he didn't want to. One time I even linked my arm in his and pressed a little and said, "Are we really here?" Boy lit up a cigar in the lab and just let the smoke out his mouth like a chimney. In the dark I could see the outline of his pick sticking out the front of his afro.

So I asked him, "Do you want my loving now, baby?"

So he waited a moment and pulled me by the hand over to a table with glass jars and beakers on it. There was a row of fat glass cylinders. When he went to turn on the light, I saw little baby mice bodies in the cylinders. They were just little baby mice floating in gray water. They were holding their hands in prayer.

Boy Commerce said, "If you have this kid, it might come out all twisted and small like this, Toya. Why you want to do some nasty shit like that?"

He said, "Toya, you think you gonna trap me like this baby here? You gonna tie my hands up? Well, *think again.* That's some stupid-ass shit. And you're a stupid-ass girl." It looked for a second like he was going to put his hand on one of the cylinders.

His eyes were red-lined. By accident, the basketball under his arm slipped out and fell on another table and knocked a beaker to the floor. "You see what you made me do, asshole?" He swept the broken pieces under the table with his foot. The smell of something fierce hit my nose, but it wouldn't make me do something stupid like cry. That was the way to lose them. Wives in school didn't cry. They just carried their load and thought their thoughts just like old women. I didn't say a word. Silence was the golden plan.

Boy switched off the light and opened the door. "Toya, get this fact through your head: I won't let you end my fucking life. I always thought you were smart."

Silence.

"So forget it, bitch. You ain't nothing but a animal." He left.

But he never said he wouldn't change once the baby got

here. He had turned off the lights and I was alone in the dark lab. I slipped off my shoes and put my hands just like the praying babies and thought: God, I do love him. Let him recognize my love for what it is. Let him follow Roc's example of loving love.

Then I let my own damn self out.

Boy is the ship, I am in the hold. Mrs. Mary taught us in history that that was how the slaves traveled. They couldn't see the outside, they were in chains. (They could maybe hear it, though. Maybe it was a dolphin flying through the air, telling them that their iron buckles would be off in about four hundred years, and maybe they were grateful for that dream from the fish. They might've even got so happy, they woulda wanted to kiss each other, this shit wasn't going to be forever, but the chains wouldn't reach, so the one who was able to slip the chains went around kissing the others for joy. She kissed their feet. That made them more together. But then the smell was bad.)

Mrs. Mary told us that the slaves had been a primitive people. That's why they didn't rebel — they had been too primitive. And sure, they had the hardships of slavery to endure before them, but that would be only a short chapter in their history, and then they would be free! Mrs. Mary said that Negro people in our country had always had it so much better than the Africans that were still in Africa. Some of them still didn't even live in houses. The Negro has definitely come a long way in America. The Negro has become — *sophisticated.*

All I knew was that Bri was wrong. I couldn't have no African name. I had me my slave name, and I wasn't going away from it never.

· · ·

Bri called me up all hysterical and shit, and I wanted to say: Like I don't have enough of my own problems, but I didn't say that. She cried so hard I thought the phone would melt.

"Toya," she whimpered, "what if I wake up one day and realize I don't love Roc?" Her crying was impossible. We had agreed not to do it.

I said, "Bri, calm the hell down. You haven't come to that point. Wait till you get married before you start in with all the soap opera shit. By that time you will need to have an affair, maybe we can fix you up with Big Daddy Dave." I was still grateful to him for that night in the lab.

She screamed, "But I don't love Roc *now!* The day in the future was this morning, and the baby throw-up almost choked me! Fuck!"

I told her to calm the hell down, but secretly I was afraid. Bri had heard about a place that would get rid of it almost at the same time it could be born, and she was going around school trying to get the information. She didn't have to become a school wife, I had told her before, because she could just *be* with him and *be* his woman. But she had to go through with the kid. How the hell could she have her anchor if she backed out now? And Roc was a white boy, an ugly one by white girl standards, flat nose and a caved-in chest, only he had this thing for Bri's hair when it wasn't relaxed, just natty afro and shit, and he had this thing for her African ass, and logically we all knew that that meant he would be easier to keep. Even the cheerleaders knew it, even if they were too stuck up to admit it. That white boy was not going back.

"Bri, just think about it for a moment. He won't ever make you work a day in your life. All he will want is children. Baby, most people would say you got it made."

She must a fallen out her seat because the phone hit the floor and I could hear her sniffling close by. "Toya, he told me that he got me pregnant on purpose, that I didn't have a damn thing to do with it! He wanted to have me forever! That's some sick shit! I don't want his fucking hands to touch me again. I'ma throw me down the bleachers at school."

I said, "It doesn't matter who got who. Point of the matter is, you got the prize at the end of the rainbow. You got your whole life ahead of you."

Bri whispered, "I don't want his fucking hands to touch me."

I ain't your goddamn vacation home! You think you can come and go if you like? YOU THINK I'MA ALWAYS BE HERE? Look me in the eye! I got feelings, too. You think you can come and go and it ain't gonna make me break inside? No, don't be looking at me like that! I got pride, damn you, and I got me, yeah that's right, ME! And it's about time I took care of me! Yeah, I know you been fucking with Margarita Santamaria, and I know she told you she came after the first time! Well, that's bullshit! It's hard for girls to come, they only say that to make you feel like a man! Yeah, I'd like to see you try and make me come! Try it! Just remember: when you're done, you ain't gonna have me to push around no more. That's not how my mama raised me! She raised me with good loving! What you talking about: good loving? Is that what you been wanting all this time? Good loving from a good woman?

Well, baby, that's what I been offering you all this time, you just been too blind to see. Let me love you. Let me show you what loving is all about. It's all in here, just for you. Just relax on me. Let's you and me reciprocate. Let me be sure. Let's reciprocate. You don't have to make me come, neither.

Boy Commerce wrote a poem for the school newspaper. Well, that was about the craziest shit I ever heard! He don't even know how to spell, and he hates English class! He hates books and he hates using your brains to do what you can do with your mouth in two seconds flat.

He wrote a poem, and he had all the cheerleaders sighing in the hallway. Bet they wished they was in my shoes.

FOR YOU

I want to say
but then I stop and think
Did you think I
could keep this song
in the bottom of my heart
with my everlasting love?
Don't keep me
let me run my wild manly course free.
I'm just an ordinary man,
doing all I can.
Wandering around
till it's true love I found.
Where's my future?
Is it you?
I'm a bird
but you want to be the sea.
So let me spread my wings, you done
    yours.
Let's stay that way
And I'll never forget you down there
If you ever learn to forget me.

Mother, Mother, Mother, Mother.

(I want you.
    I am in the ship.
    I need you.)

(This was the beginning of my own poem. I would never show it to anybody cause there ain't anybody.)

I don't want a African name. I know we should be proud. Bri calls herself "Assata" and when she isn't thinking about the future, she is feeling proud like there is something else to live for. I know we should be proud.

But face it, why don't you? Here Mr. Hancock is telling me that I could get a vocational diploma and go on to do work in food service like he used to say I could do when I was back in his class reading *Tale of Two Cities* and not paying attention really. Here he is. He said, "Toya, you still have a chance for an okay future, you don't have to throw it all away." Right? Only a primitive person would turn their nose, like I did. *Right?* Fuck Mr. Hancock. Shit, I knew damn straight I wanted a better future than in food service.

Slave of a slave. I don't want a African name. I'll keep my slave name.

Boy was voted Most Valuable Player. Margarita Santamaria was voted Homecoming Queen. Bri went and had the secret abortion but promised me she would always be my friend. Big Daddy Dave asked her to check out a private party at his crib and she said yes she would sneak out her mother's house at four A.M. in the morning. Mr. Hancock asked me if I would want Boy's newspaper poem dedicated to me in the year-book, as someone had anonymously requested, and I said, What the hell, it's his loss. Roc called me up late one night at Uncle Marion's and asked me if he could start coming over and shit, and I said, Why the hell not? Sam the cheerleader came up with Katherine as the godname. She is down with the program. She and I are going over to Tinytown's next week to check out what's new and happening.

tiger-frame glasses

The squad was made up of three girls from a school. The girls names was Debbie, Donna, and Shenay. They was stalwart, steady, and statuesque, always going round not hurting old people or weak boys but helping them. They strolled down Ronald Drive and Cahill Street to Nathalie Avenue to way over to Jefferson Estates, where they could be invited in some Body's house for cookies and where they could automatically spot trouble. Things that needed correcting. A yelling mother. A father that liked to observe things too much. A brother that was in danger of getting left back in school with a bunch of stupids. A sister that didn't have no friends and was going to get murderized by some others and furthermore she thought she was going crazy. For instance. That was at day.

At night they came together and decided Who Should Benefit From Our Good Deeds? They all had Good Hearts. They was all big strong girl students that did science superbly smart and got into the honor roll just from their math grade. You Know Girls Can Be Boy Smart. The Helper Squad was loved by every Body in Amity-ville. They was a home for girls and boys that had secrets and that needed things corrected.

The Helper Squad mothers and fathers wanted the girls to be stupendous.

(That's how I made them in my notebook. Stupendous.)

Their mothers and fathers let them talk about babies and how babies came, just as long as they don't have none of their own. Right now you all just help and do right. We love you just like you are. And don't forget: You are the Ones.

(That's how I made them.)

They had us in a circle of two, all by ourself, them close to where the bus comes, me and Bethi in a circle by ourself, but then they broke it up by telling Bethi that I had called her a slow girl in Mr. di Salvo's class yesterday so then I was an only circle. They told her Come Stand Over Here By Us. Bethi looked at me with her mouth hanging open, nothing new. She went over to the back opening of their circle. Then it was just me to make a circle out of one person, waiting for the bus which would surely include more agony. Bethi and I were apart, but together by radar we were waiting to get to Park Avenue Elementary and by radar remembering when my head got massacred in a fusillade of blood by Bibi and Crater and Martha and Bellerina last summer on this very corner. We listened to their ugly brains and their ugly ways. I wanted them like my whole Body was fire.

— I'm going with Charlie to the Back. I am his world.

— What you doing there? No one is suppose to be in the Back.

— None of your fucking business.

— The Back is where the lezzies go. You a homo.

— Teeny, tell your sister she's butt-ugly. You cunnyling-ling.

— What's that mean?

— Look in the mirror.

— No one is suppose to be in the Back. They say that's where girls.

— Look in the mirror.

They would giggle like monsters and it would fill in all the air that I had saved up in my head. I was trying to be self-independent and breathe my own air. My notebook was in my bag with all my stories in it and was my own air. I had learned about Indians in the Nineteenth Century being self-independent, especially when the Frontiersmen had it out with them over all the harms they were causing. The wagon trains moved in a circle and pulled out shotguns under the flaps. The Pioneers suffered. They had a dream. That one day this nation will rise up. The Pioneer People built America because they would not let their dream get stoppled. I learned from Mr. di Salvo that the Indians could be awful quiet, holding in their breath in the shrubberies when ambush was near. The Pioneer People would be sitting in the wagon train with women and children, some who could read and write. But they could not make out the thunder in the ground or the smoke signals from the rocks that said: You was born to sacrifice for this great land.

I do the same in my circle.

Ass. Asshole. Cunny. Four Eye Fuck. Think You a Brainiac, but You is a fucking Re-Tard. You and Your Fucking Notebook Full of Lies. (Why you have to write lies like that?) You and You Re-Tard Sister. I'ma Kick Your Goddamn Ass. Like I did Last Summer Remember. You better stay indoors. WITH YOUR NOTEBOOK. Slow Girl will be a Dead Girl. Yeah I'm Looking at You. Four Eye Fuck.

The other girls giggle gigantic giggles. Then Bellerina's sister Gimlet and her girl *friend* Big Susie come by on their way to high school and just stand there, letting the girls look them up and down. Every Body drinks in Gimlet and Big

Susie and knows in their heart that they are the rulers, even if no Body is allowed to say what else they are. Bethi is just standing there not doing a thing. Because it wasn't *her* head that got massacred last summer, the braids all torn up, the teeth in shatters. The eyes in a clump. No writing hand at all. All because of the notebook I keep with the stories. Only the girls from the bus stop think it was all about them which it was not. Bethi doesn't know what she is doing there in the girls circle. I make a note to myself that I will have to explain that to her later on. That and a thousand other things like how to be good friends with the teachers. The ones that can still be outraged and feel for you.

I watch their mouths. I try to listen with my eyes close. I can see Gimlet yanking her sister Bellerina by the hair telling her You Better not be Doing It, then lighting up a cigarette in front of every Body and then passing it to Big Susie who runs her tongue along the cigarette before she takes it in her lips and smiles back at Gimlet. From where I am standing, the girls mouths move to things that don't make any sense, like Teeny's mouth saying over and over, I want visitor hands of cyclone skirt, I want visitor hands of cyclone skirt. Every Body laughs. Which shrinks my only girl circle. Gimlet looks over in my direction but she don't do anything. Big Susie says, Yall ain't supposed to play like that. That supposed to be your fren! Only she knows it ain't playing. Something will happen that will get my ass kicked again. The other girl circle wants me in-tense. Gimlet puts her hand in Big Susie's jeans behind pocket and she and her keep on walking to the high school. I hold my breath. We watch till they're a speck. I turn my eyes down. I feel what they want. Out under the new tiger-frame glasses I'm wearing there is a world of uncovered things like hands, hair, voices, teeth, windows, behinds, desires.

. . .

(They were the most perfect girls I could think of.)

Debbie, Virgo, her favorite color was red, like the setting sun over the mountains you could see from her bedroom window. She was precise, innocent, shy, perfectionist, of service to others. Solicitous. The time she wanted to go with Donna's brother's best friend but her good virtuous held her down. All the times she got a 100 grade in math class, but she didn't say nothing. She was modesty carnation.

Donna was in love with her brother's best friend. He loved her back although he was secretly more in love with Debbie. But there are some bonds and some promises that are stronger than the Heart Dictation. There is Honor. There is Friendship. There is another Girl Truth.

Donna, Aries, was a grade A student and the most beautiful girl in the school. Sometimes rash, sometimes thorny, but always up front. Everyone wanted to say that Cynthia Wiggins was the most beautiful, but secretly they knew that beauty is not just outwardly. No, what about all that on the inside? And Donna's biggest wish in life was to become a veterinarian and take care of sick injured horses.

At the Divine Confabulation Private School For Girls Donna asked to play a slave in the Thanksgiving Assembly in the fifth grade. Everyone wanted to be a Mistress on a plantation, but Donna knew right from wrong. She was her mother and father pride and joy. Her favorite colors was brown and white.

In school Mr. di Salvo asks me if I can spell the word appreciate. If I can spell it correctly, I will get to be one of the Women in the Pioneer play. I will get to sing "This Land is Your Land" with the other Women. I will get to have Mrs. Shea from third grade sew me a bonnet and a long apron to wear over my clothes when I walk along the stage with the others. All this for appreciate on our weekly spelling bee.

Bellerina sees that I am having trouble. She and I are at the middle desk. She has not had her hair braided in days. There are all these little nubs down the back of her neck. The Ultra-Sheen grease that her mother told her to put in missed her hair and smacks down her neck and shows my reflection in it. I can almost see my corduroy pants on her neck through my tiger-frame glasses that everyone makes fun of and calls me F.E.F. cause they know I won't do nothing. I only have one pair of pants. My parents say that we are poor, but not to go out broadcasting that information. How can I help it? My knees are run down. Every Body knows. And I can't do nothing. But the school bus on page 2 of the spelling book honks to me: appreciate, appreciate. The Boloney Butcher for B whispers, I *appreciate* a truly smart girl like you. I am going stark raving for a girl in the fifth grade who is going to get it later on from the girls at the bus stop. A whole bunch of dreams. I want to do something. Will my parents finally go away with us on vacation to the mountains or the seaside like they promised? Will they send me and Bethi to private school — where we *really* belong? A truly smart girl. My brain remembers the melody lane from the day before in the backyard: Daddy mowing the dried up lawn and whistling "California Dreamer" and Mom singing the commercial for Eight O'Clock Coffee and Bethi trying to get all the words to "Shakeit Shakeit Shakeit" in one line, like there are no other words to the whole song. Me sitting in the bushes with my notebook which is the dream weavill and trying to get it all down the way I would truly like it to happen and looking up in the sunlight and wishing I had a real mother and a real father and a real sister that wanted the utmost best for me, who realized all the dynamite I have in me, like a princess or a very smart and beautiful princess/girl/student. I listen. I want to shout to Bethi, "We're going to the country, We're going to the fair" as those are the other words, but she is really too slow to get anything. I hate her.

Bellerina whispers in my ear A-P-P-R-E-S-H-E-A-T-E. I repeat her words. I want to stand in the girls circle. When I *used* to be there, Bellerina used to play the funniest jokes on me, and I wouldn't get mad. She had told Bibi in secret exactly *where* it would hurt the most on my Body to hit me, and she was right. She stold my notebook to see the stories I wrote in it so she could give the others more ammunition. She informed me that she would get her older brother Beanie from prison to take me to the Back and feel my nubs under my dress. She did all this and still. I want to stand in the girls circle. I will spin Bethi out, cause she really don't know what it means, the circle. She don't know that I should have what she has, only she don't recognize that for her genuine slowness.

Mr. di Salvo announces that I will be one of the people pulling the wagon across the prairie. They had those too, you know, when the horses died, and the cattle broke down. I don't have to wear a dress if I don't want to. The girls wearing aprons and bonnets will have to wear a dress under. But I can wear whatever I want to, even my gym suit, as a puller.

The songs I will have to sing with the chorus are "Fifty Miles on the Erie Canal." "Sweet Betsy from Pike." "Carry My Back to Ole Virginny." I will have to walk slow like they did in the old days. They did not run across the prairie. I will have to learn my songs good. Bellerina holds her big teeth under her big hand. She will get to be a Pioneer Woman. She will get a bonnet and an apron. She will get to sit in the wagon while the boys and some unlucky girls pull it. Even though she weighs as much as a ninth-grader one ton and she is butt-ugly.

The teacher is not expecting nothing. I was born on Easter, an Aries baby, so that makes me the kind that is innocent yet secretly commanding. I raise my hand and I get up slowly out my desk. My palms are sweaty. My long braids that I hate for my mother to make on me are messed up already because I've been putting my head down on my boring speller too much. I get up. The gray venetian blinds on the big window hold back the sun with their straight arms and tell me that I am in the right lane. Go on Girlie, they cheer! They reach down and pat my head like I'm the faithful dog. The door frame gets ready to move. The tiles on the floor are shivery with delight. Shakeit Shakeit Shakeit. Shakeit all you can. I open my mouth. "Bellerina Brown is a Fucking Ass. Hole." The class goes wild. Shakeit all you can. Shakeit like a milkshake, and do the best you can. The venetian blinds nod yes you can and the clouds outside fall into the classroom and swirl my brains up in a pudding. Bellerina swings for my stomach, but I land on Mr. di Salvo's desk, where I hide with the other butterflies under the stack of math tests from last Wednesday. A staunch stunning wind from the spelling lists stampedes the stalactites on my hands. Bellerina punches but I am too fast. I'm always out her way.

With both eyes open under my tiger-frame glasses I see the pretty *one hundred* girls who are in shock and who don't want to consider me anymore for them. The rough *zero* girls have questions for me later: *we ain't know you was like us, Glory!* The snaggle tooth boys cheer Hip Hip, and Boo-Boo claps me on the back. Mr. di Salvo takes me and Bellerina out the play. We will have to sit in Mrs. Shea's class with the third-graders while the assembly is on. We will have to write out the words to "The Star Spangled Banner" ten times and maybe get locked in the closet, which is Mrs. Shea's specialty.

Bellerina looks me up and down. — Later, Today, After-school. Your Ass is Grass.

I sit back in my seat. The pencil groove on my desk smiles and asks me, Now that wasn't so hard, was it?

(The story goes on.)

Shenay is a Scorpio. She do not bother with boys at all. She is sexy, strategic and silent. She figures things out. Shenay has one mission on her mind: Find those who need help, and send in the Helper Squad. That would be her, Donna and Debbie. They all live on the same street and at night, they are all dedicated to saving.

Shenay can open her bedroom window and get the feel of the ocean waves crashing against the rock. She teaches Donna and Debbie. She tells them to look behind what you see. Look for the genuine-ality of a thing. Donna and Debbie say I don't get it. Shenay says, "Let me give you an example."

When she is lying in her bed at night, she sees gypsy moths fistfighting in the wall and hears pumpernickel swans discussing yesterday's math problems together. Did you get this one? Sure. That one was a cinch. The swans kiss her on the forehead. Honey, you ain't never told us you were such a smartie.

Shenay says, "Look."

On my way to the principal's office to get my punishment okayed I pass Bethi's classroom and wave to the teacher, Mr. Flegenheimer. Can she come out right now? I just got an important message from our mother and I just want to tell her it in the hall, Mr. Fleg. Private. It's important from our mother.

Mr. Flegenheimer brings Bethi out because he is getting too many complaints from the parents of special ed that he is not treating their kids like regular human beings. That he is holding back their bathroom and making them pee in their chairs and sit in it for a long time before calling the nurse and the janitor. That he is closing the venetian blinds and making them sit there, just like that, so he can put his head down on the desk. Mr. Flegenheimer is trying to look different now, but we all know.

— You can talk for three minutes, and I mean three minutes, Glory. I have a good mind to talk to your mother on the phone to confirm this, Mr. Flegenheimer says. Then he is gone back to the class that is howling over something. His eyes are closed.

Bethi is afraid to look at me. She just got allowed into the back of their circle this morning. She is afraid of what I will do to her. Don't worry about that till later, I assure her. I will get you back later. Right now I want you to do me a favor. I want you to go to Mr. di Salvo's classroom and tell him to send Bellerina to your classroom, Mr. Flegenheimer's orders. Can you do that? Okay Bethi? Can you do that? I whisper all this to her, but it takes a real long time before she gets the directions straight. She is not a retard. She is just slow. Her whole classroom is full of slow kids, so she don't feel so alone. They get beat up all the time, except for the large ones that are truly brainless and that can kill you just by looking your way.

Bethi goes to my classroom and gets Bellerina who calls her Stupid Ass and Brick Brain all the way back to Mr. Flegenheimer's door. I'm waiting there. Martha Madison suddenly appears out of nowhere humming her group of Women's song for Assembly "I'se Gwine Back to Dixie." She says in my direction, You Gonna Wish You Was Dead Meat. Martha is cross-eyed so she sometimes scares me and she sometimes doesn't. Now I am only thinking of my plan. Bellerina slaps her five and then Martha books. Bellerina turns and looks me dead in the eye. There, I am there. Shakeit Shakeit.

The door opened to show the first victim in need: old Mrs. Goodwin, a faithful soul who had a heart of gold. She was a white lady who trusted everyone. She lived all by herself in the black neighborhood of Tar Hill where people live in apartments instead of normal houses. She can make you believe in mankind all over again. Hallelujah for Mrs. Goodwin!

She had fell down her apartment steps and all the food stamp cans of food in her grocery bag rolled into the alleyway where Joe the town bum was laying. "Help me Joe!" she cried, but he only cried back, "Mrs. Goodwin, indeed I wish I could! I myself am too weak to do much of anything." So they both agonized in tribulations until around the corner came — the Helper Squad!

Debbie helped the old bitty to her feet, but when she found that Mrs. Goodwin couldn't walk, she carried her in her girl arms up the steps to her house and put her in the bed. Donna said, "Debbie, how come you got so strong?" Debbie didn't want to say. Modesty carnation.

Donna placed all the cans of food in their cabinets and to top it off, she cooked Mrs. Goodwin a whole dinner. Saucy Frank Supper with corn and tomatoes in it. Mrs. Goodwin closed her wrinkly eyes with tears of joy. "What would this world be without girls like you?" Donna shaked her beautiful hair and made Mrs. Goodwin feel better just by looking at her.

Meanwhile Shenay was in the alleyway helping Joe the bum to his feet. He smelled strange and warm. She was telling him, "See, if you believe in yourself, you can do it." Joe said he had never believed in himself before today. He was going downtown to get a job at the local school, doing any-thing. He wants to better himself. Maybe he can raise to a janitor. Shenay, you are a gold mind. *Let me* thank *you.*

"Don't thank me. Thank the Helper Squad. We want the world to be the place where you can dream and come true."

"I need *to thank you Shenay.*"

"*I said* don't, *old man.*"

Back then. The daylights whipped out of me. I said I couldn't take it no more. I felt a rippliness in my head from the punches and slides. I told them that I would never tell on them and besides my family has a pool table in our basement. Come over and use it any time. We just don't have some things that go with it. I'll never tell on you. Come over any time. But my head was getting pulverized, and in reality I was already on a cloud floating up to the sky. The voices around said, You ain't got no pool table, Your family is poor as dirt, Don't you go on putting on airs. My lips realized, How did you know that word: *airs?* Then my head got completely mashed up. Meanwhile Beanie, Bellerina's brother, waved to me from his car and laughed because it was truly funny seeing the smartass skinny one with the spy notebook of no-good gossip bout everyone on this block get the daylights whipped out of her and maybe he even saw what I wrote about a guy like him in my notebook about how strong and handsome but feeling up ladies now what a shame and why do they have to do that when all they have to do is ask and surely someone will say, Yes Please.

Bibi and Martha had my head in a lock, and then Crater had the stupendous idea of putting me between the cinder blocks to see if they could make a girl sandwich. Bellerina said, It hurts the most when something hard is lying on top of your moist spot. The other girls looked at her funny. *Where the heck is that?* Bellerina turned her head away. She said into the wind, Why am I the only one who ever knows anything.

It did not get that far. They slabbed me on a cinder block and I felt the blood bath behind my braided head go into my braided eyes and the true way Beanie's snout nose looked came clear in my mind. Spread out like a father's but he was only a guy. Even with that snout nose I saw through to Beanie's handsomeness. Didn't I say so in my notebook? Next to the made up stories about Debbie Donna and Shenay there was this gorgeous guy named B. who went to prison but who was really too handsome to really do anything prisonable. He was in secret a millionaire and he was going to fix a deserving girl up in private school where they learn. Only in real life now his car says Dodge. He is handsomely driving a Dodge. Away. I felt like laughing and then the blood trinkled to the line that was my mouth, all the way into my neck, later my eyelids. The blood burned deeper the spot of lonely that was already there. We have a pool table. Only problem is we don't have the balls that go with it. Where is every Body running? Why are you going? Wait. But it was too late. I was there half a sandwich for a pillow and no way in hell Beanie in his Dodge was going to give me another look now.

At the bus stop I am always shrinking of the girls. Fall Spring Morning Bedtime Schoolclothes PJs. I want to be with them but I am also shrinking. I wish I was dumber. I wish I was getting left back. I wish I weighed a hundred twenty pounds in the fifth grade. Then I would be in the bus stop circle. I could stop feeling Bethi breathe down my plaid dress in her waiting. She stands so close. I need to do something to her, even though she will never tell on me, and that fact makes it more stupider to do it in the first place.

My mother thinks that I am incomprehensible for wishing these kinds of things. To be left back and big. My father just laughs in the background, while he is watching *60 Minutes*. He laughs, Just one look at Glory's math grades and you can tell she's gonna be in the fifth grade a long time, maybe years. I would of got a horse whipping. You don't know how easy things are nowadays. It's the state of cultural illiteracy. Then he goes back to watching. Mother adds, And another thing: You better stop bringing up private school, girl. It's just incomprehensible. Do you think we made out of money? Then Father adds, And you better stop writing in that damn notebook and write something for Mr. di Salvo that will get you passed into sixth grade. Bethi smiles at me but I don't want it. Then they go on. Mother is folding clothes and telling Bethi what to put down on her spelling worksheet and my father is saying to the tv I Been Told You That Last Year Stupid Ass and I am doing nothing important, just standing there in an invisible cloud of butterflies, roaches, and wasps, all asking me to be their best friend.

Bellerina looks me up and down in the hallway. — What you doing here?

Before I can open my mouth she says: You want me to permanently damage that shit-ass face of yours?

— Bellerina, let's you and me go to the Back. No one will know.

— Now what in Shit's Heaven do I want to go to the Back with you for? You ain't no Body. Forget it. I'ma kill you.

— Aww no, Bellerina, I have something really big to tell you out there. If you know this you will be Boss of the Girls. You will have the Power.

— What in Shit's Heaven?

— Please come with me. Then you can whip my ass in front of the whole school. Let's run to the Back. Okay? Let's run. Let's run.

Debbie ran across little Tiffany Hammond. Tiffany was in tears, and her brown curls glittered in the sun. "What is the matter, dear child?" Debbie asked. Tiffany said it was all these words she couldn't get on her spelling quiz. She was going to fail third grade. She couldn't even make up a spelling story. She sat on the steps of her apartment and wept perfoundly. Debbie put her arms around Tiffany.

"Let me help you," she said. By magic, Donna came with Shenay. The two of them explained spelling tips to little Tiffany. They taught her how to practice to win. Meanwhile Debbie thought of a story that could put together the words Gather Garnish Gaze Gazebo Generous Generosity Genuine Ghost Gibberish. They read Tiffany's story out loud and they laughed in harmony. Tiffany said, "You saved me from impending doom, all you are geniuses" and they laughed when they realized that Genius was a spelling word too.

Shenay said why don't we start a spelling club at school cause she said girls need to know more spelling words than boys so that they wouldn't be sitting on no steps in the middle of the day crying their goddamn eyes out. "Girls can be strong, Tiffany. Tears ain't always the answer." Shenay said. Donna said that a spelling club would be just fine. Donna said that she had something to discuss with Debbie in private, so goodbye Shenay. Shenay thought a minute to herself. Then she said, "Yeah, Goodbye Girls."

Bellerina and I snuck out the window over the emergency door. I sent Bethi back to her class only I didn't know if she could make it without blabbing. Me and Bellerina walked half the way to the Back. We didn't say a word. We looked over by the handball court and saw the High Schoolers smoking there. They cursed all the time but it didn't sound like the way elementary cursed. It came over elementary lips like bowling balls except Bellerina who it was her natural way of life. High Schoolers could curse up a storm and when it was over, you realized that all they said was hi how you doing? Bellerina waved to her sister standing out there with Big Susie but they didn't notice her. Gimlet had her warm arm around Big Susie's shoulder, and their faces was really next to each other. I felt my secret long heart.

Charlie came out the shack that stood in the corner of the Back. We could see him from half way. Charlie wiped his mouth along the edges with his pointer finger and his thumb. He was big and small at the same time. He waved to us to come. "I'm feeling warm!" he shouted. He was leaning against the shack.

Bellerina looked a bit scared. She turned to me. — So what you want? What you got to tell me?

I swallowed. — Bellerina. I don't want to fight anymore. What is it about me you don't like? I can change! My notebook is only stories. Of how things can maybe be. I am really smarter than people think. I can change! Bellerina!

— I don't like your fucking face. Can you change that?

I also don't like your slobbering re-tard sister. Why she have to stand with us?

I also don't like it you think you are better than me. You think you a Brainiac. Well let me tell you. That's a damn lie. Write that in your damn notebook full of lies. Four Eye Fuck In Liar. You hurt a lot of people with them damn lies. That's what you are.

Bellerina walked away just like that. So my plan had failed.

I just kept my head down and my eyes closed. Bellerina walked to the shack. It was a stupid plan when you got right down to it.

I sighed with the future. Your Body never gets used to it. It hurts more each time. I de-test the feeling of hands messing me up. I am a girl made out of brown peel, not iron and steel. I also de-test the eyes. They can mess you in a way that makes you afraid to sleep at night, get up in the morning. The eyes can push you off into a lonely circle, like the circle of me and my sister, like the circle of me. I de-test it all.

Bellerina called back to me — I'ma get you this afternoon. Me and the girls. You better be ready. Drag me out in the cold. You lucky Charlie is here for me.

She went with Charlie in the shack. Charlie said "Dag! Dag!" and I saw other High Schoolers fastwalking there. She had said: I'm his whole world.

Bellerina's sister Gimlet shook her head when she saw Bellerina going in the shack. Big Susie grinned. Gimlet usually doesn't care, even when she swears she will kick anyone's butt who messes with her little sister. She took a puff of cigarillo, down to her feet. She looked and shaked her head. Big Susie laughed, "She's going to get *lit up.*"

They were needed again. Little Bobby Lee had fallen off his sister's banana seat bike and was bleeding. Another boy stood near him. "Help!" the big boy cried. Soon a crowd was there. No one was capable of doing nothing. Lucky for them Debbie, Donna and Shenay was speeding on their way to the place.

"What happened?" Debbie asked. The big boy told her. The crowd agreed. Bobby was so clumsy when you weren't looking. His sister was in tears.

Shenay stepped up and looked at the big boy. She waited a moment with eyes that didn't move. She said, "I'm waiting." The crowd growed silent. The sun didn't move from the sky. She said, "I'll wait." The big boy looked. A river of pee ran down his leg and he bawled. "It was not all my fault," he bawled.

Shenay stepped back. The crowd laughed and started smacking the big boy upside his head. Someone held little Bobby Lee in their arms and rocked him to sleep like a scared hummingbird. Shenay stepped back until she was just a speck on the distance.

I sat down on the steps of the handball court, and out the stretch of my eye, I could see the shack at the Back. High Schoolers went in and they stayed. The sky hung blue. Gimlet walked over to me out of nowhere. I had to catch my breathing. I was thinking about burning my notebook. It was just a bunch of stories. A fire would prove something. Or I could take cinder blocks and make a sandwich. That would be better proof.

Gimlet stopped in front of me and said she heard I was going to get my ass kicked. That's what she heard. She looked over at the shack. She shrugged her shoulders. But then she just kept on walking, like the air was not holding her down.

Shenay called a special meeting. It was at her family's ski lodge, and her parents were both away on a medical mission in the Heart of Africa. "I want to speak to you both from my soul," she explained to the girls.

She pulled Darnell Williams out her closet. "Is this the boy you two been dreaming about?" The girls nodded yes. "Well, stop it right now. We have a large mission at hand. What will happen if we don't save things?" The two others didn't have anything to say in their shame. "What will happen if we ain't responsible for the lips and knees and heads and hearts of others?"

Shenay took Darnell Williams and kissed his mouth into her own. She put his face on her chest and said, "There. Ooh there." She told him, "Also: Kissing me on my neck drives me wild. Now you going to have to give me what you been giving these two." There was no arguing with Shenay.

The other two said, "We understand" and went on home to do their social studies homework. They realized that Shenay could have it all, but she was doing this to be responsible. She taught them a uplifting lesson about girls in the life of the world.

In the corner of my eye I saw Bellerina fastwalk out the shack in the Back. She was saying something but then Charlie pulled her back in. Her shirt was open. I could see the sides of it blowing in the wind. I could see that she was not wearing a undershirt but a womanly brassiere.

In the hallway Gimlet was talking to Principal Blackburn. Big Susie was nodding yes to everything. Gimlet cried, And if my goddamn sister can't be learning here in school I'ma go to the damn super-in-ten-den to get some answers. You suppose to be watching over these kids. And they hanging all over the place who knows where doing shit.

Principal Blackburn said, Gimlet it's good that you watch out for Bellerina. She's been having trouble. Why hasn't your mother called? Or your father? We need your parents to take action.

— I'm her parent. Shit. I'm just as good.

— This is really the job of a father, Gimlet. You are pretty young yourself. Please send your father in to see me.

— You see Big Susie? Well, she is Bellerina's father, if I say so. Get that through your thick head, Mrs. Blackburn. Shit.

Shenay pushed Darnell Williams out a five story window. His Body was a blood bath. She didn't have time for that kind of mess. She knew there was more important things in life besides girls loving boys. Why do girls always be helping others? Why don't girls grow up to be mad scientists? Why don't girls grow up and love other girls and fight over them instead of boys? The world had too many fences in it for Shenay. She called the ambulance to come and pick up the blood bath.

Mr. di Salvo came outside and grabbed my shoulder. Bethi was next to him, looking guilty in her slow way. She knew I was going to fix her. Mr. di Salvo asked, "What the hell are you doing out here?" pulling me back into Park Avenue. He dragged me past Gimlet and Mrs. Blackburn. Mr. di Salvo listened and took out his hanky and wiped the sweat off his lip. "Hell," he said.

He turned to me. "You are lucky your sister blabbed. You trying to get your butt beat? Always looking for a way out of math. You barely passed the test from last Wednesday. But just how would you know that, Glory? You just sitting out here enjoying the day when the rest of us are looking over the math answers. You. You. You. You. You."

I looked at my sister before we dumped her off at Mr. Flegenheimer's. I could not think of any big evil to scare her with. She blinked at me. I growled, What you want, Bethi? Stop wasting my precious time. Stop looking at me. Wipe your nose. Close your damn mouth.

But Bethi put her nose close to my shoulder. She sniffed me. She whispered so only I could hear, I don't want you get beat up Glory. I going to help you. We going to poison them. We going to kill them so we can stand back together. I want to be with you. We going to make poison.

I stopped. I hugged my sister. I didn't care. I hugged her till we got to Mr. Flegenheimer's, where the kids were screaming like gorillas from behind the door. Mr. di Salvo made me let her go.

Shenay didn't let her mind go down, like some other girls she knew. She concentrated. When she saw a girl, she did not try to explain it that the wind or the stars or the pencils told her to do it. She did not have to go crazy in her head to feel the genuine things. She walked up to the girl and held her in her arms and said, "You are my present to me." That's all there was to it. She would always help Those In Need, Shenay would. She did not have to be a nutcase.

Big Susie saw me and walked next to me on the way back to Mr. di Salvo's class. Mr. di Salvo held my arm tight. He was thinking about how I had been a different girl. That meant *zero* girls punishment. But by the time we got to our classroom, Mr. di Salvo was thinking of letting me be in the chorus to sing one of the assembly songs. He said I would have to learn the words and not just goof off with my head in the clouds like I am prone to do. Could I learn the words and not be a screwball. Mr. di Salvo was feeling for me and that was a good surprise.

Big Susie was walking next to me. She leaned over and her chest touched me on the shoulder. She whispered in my ear that I was not getting beat up that day or on any day. Bellerina was not going to get me. Bellerina was not going to get anyone. Big Susie touched my hair with her hand. She said, You girls are scared shitless. Then you go and do some shit. Just wait. And then Big Susie was gone.

I'se going back to Dixie
No More I'se gwine back to wander,
My Heart's Turned Back to Dixie
I can't stay here no longer
I miss de old plantation, my friends and my relation,
My heart's turned back to Dixie, and I must go.

I've hoed in fields of cotton
I've worked up on de river
I used to think if I got off
I'd go back there, no never
But time has changed de ole man, His head is bending low
His heart's turned back to Dixie, and I must go.

I sat in the desk in the back of the room, next to Martha Madison. She tried to look rough and scare me into last year, but I kept my eyes right on her till she looked away. The venetian blinds asked me how I felt. The pencil groove in my desk wanted to know why I wasn't talking to it anymore. I said out loud, I don't want you. *No more.* Martha Madison winked her eyes in the other direction trying to do like I was crazy. Only I wasn't.

You can change things just by ignoring the furniture. You can get your own kind of strength. I looked hard at Martha Madison. From the side, her eyelids had on a trace of her mother's eye makeup, Blue Oceans. Martha always stold her mother's makeup to come to school in. She had dreams. The desk wood was silent. The venetian blinds were just venetian blinds. I looked hard at Martha. I also had dreams. I will keep my notebook in my schoolbag. That's the proof. I will get back in that circle.

wonderful teen

IT SEEMED TO ME that our motel room in Laguna Beach was only big enough for two people, like a mother and father, and here we were five. Mother picked up the phone and dialed for a plain cheese pizza. We protested, saying that we wanted a pizza with mushrooms and little fishes on it, and a bottle of orange soda as well, since it was so hot. The sun outside was turning roads back into tar, and the pool at the motel was as hot as a bath. A few minutes outside, and we could feel the light brown of our skin bake darker, like brownies with nuts in them. There was my baby sister Tess and me and the twins, Todd and Lee. Lee was named after my father, who was back at the house, probably cursing out loud to no one. We ran the bathroom sink full at the motel and soaked our arms up to the elbows in the cold hard water. Sometimes someone would say, "It's too hot here in this stinking room" or "I wish we were back at home." Mother would tell us to think about something else and to behave ourselves. That, and "I'm not made out of money! You eat what I say! If you're thirsty, fill yourself up a glass from that water you're playing with!"

Mother picked up the phone again and told us to be quiet. We all sat on the edge of the bed. I held Tess on my lap. I knew that she would be the first one to start bawling, no matter what. Mother twisted a strand of her ash-blond hair around her finger and put it in her mouth. The swelling around her eye had turned dark purple from the sky-blue it had been in the morning. When we walked into the motel office at eight A.M., Mother took off her sunglasses automatically, forgetting. The old lady behind the desk stared at us. Mother asked, "Do you give discounts for black eyes?" Then she started to cry, which made us all feel very wobbly. Mother put her sunglasses back on and touched each of us, one by one, with the tip of her hand, like she was making sure we were there. The old desk lady said, "Honey, we've seen everything." She gave us the room closest to the old highway because she said she didn't want to hear no trouble. She asked my mother if she was babysitting us kids. "They are mine," Mother announced. The old desk lady said she had never seen four colored kids come in with a white lady with a black eye before. She said she wasn't looking for no trouble. Mother sucked in her teeth and moved us out the door.

In the last issue of *Wonderful Teen*, it had said that most people don't really realize how grown-up and responsible their teens really are. "Today's youth," it said, "tomorrow's *you*." That made me feel different after I'd read it, even though I was only twelve. Now, on the way to our motel room, my hand was on Mother's shoulder, not like it used to be when I was a girl, when I used to hold on to her fingers with my whole hand. I'd brought the last issue of *Wonderful Teen* with me, because before we left, Mother made it clear to us: we will stay gone.

She was trying a new number. She said to me, "Hannah,

get me a cigarette out of my bag." I pushed Tess off my lap and dug into her pocketbook for the twisted pack of Slims. *Wonderful Teen* was against cigarettes: it said that smoking could turn youthful skin not only older but darker as well. I knew this fact, and still, I never gave up my prayer with the pack of Slims in my hand that six years would hurry up and pass so that I would be able to smoke cigarettes legally, like Mother promised. It happened around the same time you could drink a chaser before your main drink and join the army and get married. My prayer was the same lines over and over: "And when I am a full woman . . . And when I am a full woman . . . thank you, heavenly God." I would start smoking nonfilters and I would be exactly like Mother anyway, who smoked all the time, and look: her skin was soft and youthful and not dark at all.

Mother lit up a cigarette and said, "Is that you, Lee?" Tess's lips began to shake so I whacked her on the head with Mother's bag, gently. Mother said, "You can't push me around now, Lee. You can't do that now! We're on the coast. Never mind where! One more word like that and I'll hang up for good!" The boys put their heads underneath the bedspread and began to howl like baby dogs. Tess was full-steam-ahead crying, just as I had predicted. I said, in the most mature adult whisper I could manage, "Shut up, you disgusting brats!"

Mother's voice was scratchy, like she was gargling with saltwater. She said, "You can't push me around now! No sir, there's not going to be a next time! There's a point I've reached, Lee, and that's called: *self-respect.*" She slammed down the phone and told us to go outside and wait for the pizza delivery truck. I shoved my brothers and sister out the door and said to my mother, still in that grown-up whisper, "You know I'm here if you need me, Ella." Mother put out her cigarette in the ashtray and said, "Just where did you learn talk like that? Go out and close the door!"

In the sun, our game was to put our hand on each other's foreheads to see who had the hottest skin. Tess wanted to change after a few minutes; she said she wanted to be a little white cloud that floated above the motel and looked at itself in the pool mirror. My brother Todd, who was only ten years old and just naturally thought he was the absolute Panama Cigar, said, "That's only something deluded baby girls think of. Me, I've had enough of delusions." Lee, still in the old game, jumped up and down and announced that his skin was on fire. I looked at them and folded my arms over my chest. Tess, Todd, and Lee were nothing but babies when you faced the cold, hard facts. I had been born two years before any of them, and in *Wonderful Teen* it had said, "Every year marks a difference." Lee said he wanted to go back in and tell Mother that he had a fever, but I said not to. I said she needed time to find herself, and Todd said, "Why, is she lost?" and he horse-laughed. I ignored him and pushed the others over to the pool.

There was a colored lady sitting next to the pool in a lounge chair. She was the first black person I'd seen all day, ever since we drove into Laguna Beach on the lam. She saw us and cried out, "Come and play your games over here by me!" She smiled. Her voice sounded like our grandma from the South, the one who wore an undershirt instead of a bra and who ate squirrel meat. The colored lady was beautiful. She had the same skin as Dad, the kind Mother had called "day-old coffee" in the old times when they used to laugh about it. The colored lady was just sitting there in broad daylight. She didn't have her arms or legs covered up in the sun. She kept batting her eyes. The look on her face was the kind that said *I'm never lonely*.

Todd and Lee went over to her and did cartwheels and rode upside-down bicycles with their legs. This colored lady's hair was made up into a thousand braids wrapped in one big twist at the back of her head. There were blue and gold beads woven into the braids. Blue and gold were my favorite colors. I suddenly remembered. Blue and gold were the national colors of *Wonderful Teen.* Todd and Lee were playing the Injured Cowboy and the Horse Who Could Dial for Help. She threw her head back and laughed. Her teeth could have been a full-page ad in *Wonderful Teen;* they had that unmistakable teen shine, although I guessed her to be a bit older. She looked over at Tess and me and said, "Are you feeling blue, girls?" Her voice was like a love story in the movies.

I shoved Tess behind me and said, "Our mother is under the weather. I am here to keep an eye out on the kids. You see, I'm almost a teen. And I'm here to keep an eye out."

The way the colored lady leaned forward in her chair, you could really see things if you looked. She tied the knot of her two-piece white-and-gold swimsuit tighter and said, "If you're going to be a teen, then you probably have all the reasons in the world for feeling blue." She winked at me. The boys ran to the highway edge to check for the delivery truck. My arms were hanging at my sides like long noodles, and suddenly I realized how amazing it was that I was going to be a teen.

The colored lady took Tess by the hand and said, "With this kind of hair, she'll have all the boys. All the boys who wouldn't want *us.*" Tess had Mother's hair, the kind that was soft and went straight down. Not like mine, which didn't flow to the back when the wind hit it. My hair just stayed.

Then the colored lady asked, "What does your mother have?"

Tess said, "Dad slammed the phone down on Mother's

hand, so that's why we're all here." She put her face in her hands, just like a grown-up, even though she was only five.

The colored lady turned and said to me, "Do you want me to start showing you the right way to be a teen?"

The boys came back and hung their legs over the side of the pool. The colored lady was braiding my hair. I sat on the ground in between her legs and looked into her compact mirror. She made five rows of braids on my head from front to back instead of the two that Mother usually did. She took out a jar of light blue grease and smoothed it through the rows over the hair that wouldn't stay put. I smelled like Dad in the morning. Tess said I looked like a star. I sat between the colored lady's legs on the hot cement and felt what *Wonderful Teen* would have called "The Evolution" come out.

The colored lady asked me, "Does your mama know what a beautiful baby she has here? You're going to get all the boys with your charm."

I said, "But what about my hair?" I asked her if I would still get all the boys with my hair. She smiled. Mother called for us from the door of the room. The colored lady wanted a goodbye kiss from the boys. I looked at myself one last time in the compact. I said to myself, "And when I am a full woman, I will always look like this. And when I am a full woman, I will always look like this. Thank you, heavenly God." Remembering our game, I shouted out to the others racing back, "Has anyone's skin reached the boiling point yet?"

Todd and Lee ran back into the bathroom to play with the water. Mother was flopped on the bed. Tess was flopped on Mother's chest and was trying to hide her face inside Mother's blouse. There were three cigarettes, all lit, in the ashtray. Mother's face looked tired and had red blobs all over it. She was wearing her sunglasses again, even though it was just us. When I sat next to her on the bed, I could smell the way our home smelled at night, when Mother smoked and cooked in the kitchen. The TV was on: it was our favorite show, *Day in Court.*

A man had returned home after twelve years of amnesia and now his wife's new husband was feeling pretty disgusted and was filing for divorce. The new husband called his wife a "black plague," and that made Todd laugh like crazy. The wife sat in the witness stand like a stone with its mouth open. She said she hadn't known. The judge said it was a clear-cut case of bigamy. The old husband just woke up in Las Vegas and adjusted to life as a children's librarian there. He'd married again, had a son, and gotten arrested for bad checks. But all that didn't matter now, now that he remembered who he really was. The new husband rolled his eyes at the camera and said, "Plague is right." The judge said it was a clear-cut case of mistaken identity.

When it came time for the wife to speak, Mother said, "Turn the set off. It's too damn late for her."

There was this ad in the last *Wonderful Teen* that I loved: a lady in a tanning studio applying a bottle of Wild Thing tanning oil to her silky legs. And she was dreaming of a man who had sun-streaked hair and closed eyes with a heavenly smile on his face. The ad said, "True Happiness." That was it. I tore it out of the magazine and kept it in my slacks pocket. Whenever I looked at it, I wanted to take off my shirt. Whenever I looked at it, first I would feel sexy, then sad.

I thought about the colored lady at the pool. I said to Mother, "Do you notice anything different about me?" I twirled the ends of my braids in my fingers.

Mother closed her eyes and said, "Not now, Hannah. Can't you see I'm thinking?" One of her eyes was glued together by the lids in a purple ball.

I told her what I was thinking, though: that now I didn't look exactly like her anymore, but still, when people looked, they would be able to tell that I was hers. Mother laughed, "Oh yeah? You sure you're not shitting me?" Then after a minute she said, "To me, you're looking more like your father's side. Are you *sure* you're still mine?" And she laughed. And her laugh was the kind that meant: I might be serious.

I ran into the bathroom and looked into the mirror. I wanted to pull all the braids out. I wanted a hat or a scarf: I was ashamed. There were five braids where there used to be two and everything felt like it was gone and I was ashamed to death. Todd walked past the bathroom and whispered, "Plague" and with both hands I slammed the door. Shut.

Todd and Lee had been playing with the water, but now they came running out of the bathroom. The sink was overflowing. Todd announced, "I want to go home now."

Mother replied, "We can't right now, honey. Be good for a while. We'll check in on Dad later."

Lee said, "I want Dad to bring me my bike."

I said, "Now you two boys *behave!* I don't want to have to tell you again." I turned to Mother and I sighed. "What's a woman to do?"

Todd said, "Shut your face, black bitch." His voice was high and shaky. He kept his eyes on Mother's feet, lying on the bed.

"Yeah, black bitch," Lee copied. He was smiling like an angel. He was clearly such a baby.

I shouted, "Mother! We don't have to stand for this!" I began to think of punishments for the boys.

She rubbed her eyes under the sunglasses and said, "Kids! That's the last thing I need! Nobody calls anybody else a black anything! Far as I am concerned, we are all *black*."

She slid off the bed and put on her slippers and walked into the bathroom. No one said anything because it was just a feeling. Mother clicked the bathroom door locked. The only noise was from the highway. You could tell that inside, everything went frozen, frozen stiff, even our teeth hurt. You could tell we were alone.

Todd fell on the bed next to Tess and started bawling. Then Lee started in. Todd wriggled his body in the covers like a desert soldier. Mother shouted after a minute, "I have so many things to worry about, don't give me anything else on my plate, you hear?"

The toilet flushed. Then Mother resumed saying, "Boys, I'm doing all I can. Ask Hannah to read you a story."

I looked at my brothers on the bed. I was thinking: Yes, it was true. Even Mother had to admit I was the natural-born leader of the children. It was all up to me. I moved over and touched Todd's back with the flat of my hand and I let it stay there for a minute. Yes, it was true. He screamed at me to get my black bitch hand away. The toilet flushed again. I moved back for a moment. Then I slid underneath the bed like a sideways crab.

The doorbell to our room rang, and it was the old desk lady. She wanted to know whether Mother was interested in buying something to drink. She was selling bottles of Old Country Gentleman at a discount price. This was the stuff that would be good for someone like our mother, she said. I told her, "We are probably going to order a bottle of orange soda, which is rich in vitamin C."

Mother was back on the phone. "I told you how to get

here," she was shouting. "Are you going to keep me waiting all damn day?" She slammed the phone down. We were all listening. "Who was that at the door?" Mother asked, going back into the bathroom.

Later, she made us wash our faces and brush our teeth even though it wasn't dark outside yet. She sat us down in a row in front of the TV and told us we could watch *Nature's Glorious Kingdom* and *The Gentle Giant*. We had to put on our pajamas. Mother combed out our hair. She asked me why mine was so greasy, but that was all. She didn't ask me where the braids came from. The doorbell rang. Lee said, "Maybe that's Dad." Todd replied, "Shut up, stupid dope."

It was the colored lady from the pool. Mother was peeking out from behind the front door. The way the lady stood in the doorway with her short white robe covering almost every important thing, I just knew she was a star. We were in Laguna Beach. That was home to the stars. The colored lady said she was selling cosmetics, natural cosmetics that didn't have any unnecessary chemicals or animal tests. They enhanced a woman's natural beauty without covering up or polluting what nature had put there in the first place.

Mother said she wasn't interested. The colored lady took out a small case from a huge bag that had "Only One You" on the side. It was a dark blue eye shadow. She said, "That one goes over big with ladies of your hue." She dabbed Mother's eyes, including the purple one. Then she said, "You'd be surprised to discover all the treasures that this particular tone can bring out." She showed Mother an orange lipstick called Debonair and a bottle of pink foundation. The colored lady said it would bring out the secret most beautiful woman that Mother had inside of her. Mother said, "I ain't in the market for that today, honey."

The colored lady gave her an eye pencil called Fire and Smoke and a mascara with a special lash-separating comb. She saw us through the door and waved. She pointed to my head and smiled. I felt my throat get thick. Mother kept her eyes down. She thanked her for the samples and then closed the door. Then the colored lady was gone, like that was all there was to it. Mother was silent. I knew that that meant *We are back in here together alone.*

She went back into the bathroom. When she came out, she had on the lipstick and the eye pencil. Her eyes looked like two wonderful stones. She asked us, "Is the treasure out?" and then burst into tears. We were all frozen again, but still we could run and put our arms around her.

Nature's Glorious Kingdom came on. I could tell that the day was ending because out the window, the bottom of the sky was turning pink. Tiny stars were popping out everywhere. *Wonderful Teen* said that the eveningtime would become a teen's best friend, what with the promise of corsages, candy, dates arriving at the door, cars, limousines, evening dresses. I sat on the edge of the bathtub and anticipated the universe as Mother scrubbed her feet and hands. She took moments out to dry her hands and smoke a cigarette. I said to her, "I wish I was eighteen already."

She answered, "Hannah, baby, when you're eighteen, you're going to wish yourself right back to twelve, believe you me." She smiled at me for the first time in days.

I thought about the car I would start driving when I hit the wonderful age, and all the men standing at street corners waiting for me to pick them up and drive them around. I would have on nylons, and instead of underwear, I would wear a white-and-gold bikini bottom. The men's hair would blow in the wind and they would have the best suntans. I would show Tess how to drive way before her time and how to hold a penny between her legs for posture. I would use Debonair.

I said, "I only want to keep getting older, Mother. I want to be exactly like you."

Mother said, "By the time I was twenty-nine, I had had all of my children. Grandmother used to call me and tell me that it was never too late. It didn't matter what I'd thought I wanted before. She just wished it could have been anything else — South American, Russian, even Chinese, for Christ's sake. I had four children, but my own freaking mother told me it was never too late to leave and come back and be twelve again."

Then Mother said, "Dad could've been anything, and still I would've fallen in love. It's not that love is blind, for Christ's sake. It's that love closes your eyes out of spite. Dad could've been anything, and still I would've gotten to right here." And then her cigarette fell out of her mouth and into the water.

I picked it up and said, "I don't care about all that other stuff, Mother. I just want to be like you."

Mother rubbed her eyes. She said, "At first your father called me his little drop of milk in his big bucket of tar."

Then she said, "And it's not like I ever became more than a drop of milk in the bucket of tar. I didn't spread out. I didn't evaporate. I just stayed a drop of milk and he just stayed a bucket."

Mother took a deep breath. I couldn't listen. I told her again that I wanted to be just like her, and she moaned, "Then be like me, Hannah."

The doorbell rang and it was the desk lady again. She said to tell Mother that there was a man around asking for her. She said she wasn't looking for no trouble, but facts were facts: someone had been sniffing around. Mother shouted from the bathroom, "Shut that damn door!" The desk lady asked me how long it was we were planning on staying. I smiled graciously to get her to leave, and then she did leave.

We turned the TV set low. We could hear Mother splashing water in the tub, saying, "It's not possible! How the hell could it be possible!" She got out of the tub and started throwing all our clothes in a big pile near the door.

The bell rang again, and this time we all looked out the window and saw the pizza delivery guy. Mother opened the door and said, "I called you hours ago! Do I need to make reservations a week in advance for a freaking pizza?"

The pizza guy said, "I got lost, that's all. No biggie." He placed a big soggy box on the floor next to our pile and began to chew his nails. He had streaked blond hair and legs with muscles. His shirt was open. He had what *Wonderful Teen* would call "that unmistakable surfer air."

The guy was eyeing Mother as she was fishing for some dollar bills. He asked her finally, "So what time do you knock off babysitting?" Mother was searching for her pocketbook. She was only wearing a towel. Tess moved over and started twirling her hair with her finger. She gave him a big smile. She was only five.

He rubbed the back of his neck with his hand. I suddenly realized that I was wearing feet pajamas, but I was praying he hadn't noticed. "And when I am a full woman, I will wear baby dolls. And when I am a full woman, I will wear baby dolls. Thank you, Father." Mother mumbled something at him and handed over a ten-dollar bill. He grinned and bent his head down to hers — did I mention that he was probably over six feet tall in his stocking feet and had five-o'clock shadow? He asked Mother if he could speak to her outside for a moment. "Why?" Mother asked, but she was already going into the bathroom with a sundress from the pile.

I sauntered over to the pizza guy. I put my hands on my hips and spread out my fingers wide so that it would look like something big and good was there. And then he stared into my eyes for a whole sixty seconds. They were as blue as Mother's new eye shadow. He put his warm hands on my shoulders, which were pulsating a feeling up to him. I was almost as tall as he was. I'd say he stared into my eyes for a good eighty seconds. I'd say that there was definitely love there.

Standing with me there, he said, "*Baby*," and he said it so that I would have to follow his lips to really know the depth of his entire being. And I felt my whole essence get crushed and I knew that this had most certainly been a *Wonderful Teen* moment. I felt the beating of my rapid heart and all my favorite songs filling my head, like "Where Is My World." They were filling my soul. Baby. I wanted to sing. Heaven was really a place you could see before you died.

And then Mother came out of the bathroom with her yellow sundress on. The pizza guy pulled his hands away quickly and said, "That's a cute girl there. Where's her mother? I mean, I know you ain't their mother." Mother stopped a second, then she burst out laughing and said, "Of course they're mine, silly. I'm old enough." She pushed him gently out the door and followed, grinning gaily.

I went into the bathroom and turned on the water. The others were watching *Gentle Giant* and tearing off pieces of pizza from the box. I began scrubbing my face with cold water and the palms of my hands. Just water and hands. I looked up in the mirror over the sink after a minute, and I thought I saw myself going, but when I blinked my eyes, I was all there.

Out the window, the moon came out in full and the air was cooling down. I used our family-size jar of Vaseline for grease and did my hair again. I couldn't get the five braids, but I did smooth my hair out more, even my girl sideburns. I got two braids down the back of my head, Indian warrior fashion.

Mother came into the room after fifteen minutes. "That boy!" she said, giggling. Her face was red, and the blobs on it were even redder. "What a crazy *boy!*" She knelt near the pizza box and tore out a slice and stuffed it in her mouth. She said, when everyone kept on watching TV, "All he wanted to do was ask me out on a date! Now isn't that a crazy *boy?*" And she let out a string of giggles that sounded like they could've come from a cow. Todd said, "This pizza is too goddamn cold," but all Mother did was grab him and start hugging him. Her face was all lit up. She looked ugly. She didn't punish him for using the wrong language. Mother grabbed Tess and Lee and began hugging them too and kissing them and pretty soon they were all rolling on the floor, happy like puppies. They were all giggling in little lumps, like on a string, not laughing in one big laugh. Mother asked, "Where's Hannah?" but they were all too happy and giggling to answer. It was the first time in a long time.

Then Mother spread her arms out like wings around Tess and Todd and Lee and said, "My babies, you are all mine." And I could hear tears in her voice. It was the saddest time I ever knew. Mother rocked them like they were all back in the nest. I closed the door to the bathroom, where I was standing, looking, and I wondered if they would ever remember that I wasn't there, ever.

Before we went to bed, Mother called Dad again. She was still wearing her sundress and her new makeup. Dad picked up, saying it was pretty damn late to be calling and did she know she was facing possible kidnapping charges? Mother put Tess on the phone, then the boys. They all cried in no time. When you faced facts, they were all nothing but children, pure and simple. When I got on the phone, I told Dad,

"I have everything under control. I'm not your baby." Then I said, "Yes. Yes, I miss you. I already told you that before." Then I said calmly, *"Why couldn't you have been something different?"* Someone here needed to get to the bottom of things. Mother smacked me hard on the back and told me to mind my own freaking business. Then she took the phone into her own hands.

Back in the bathroom, I put on Mother's eye shadow and lipstick and pink foundation. I put it on seriously. There was this article in the last issue of *Wonderful Teen* called "Dress, But Don't Confess," which said that all wonderful teens had secrets in them that should only come out with the right man. Not just any man, the absolute right one. It said that lip gloss and eyeliner and a great tan were important, but the right man didn't need too much to see all the treasures that a wonderful teen possessed. I used to believe that. Only now I didn't know what to believe anymore. I studied my face in the mirror. From the side I could still pretend. From the side I knew for sure that I resembled Mother. That was a fact as plain as day, couldn't anyone deny it. But when I looked forward in the mirror, my face was homely and alone. I didn't know if I could fully believe *Wonderful Teen.* I realized, for example, that there were no treasures, not on the outside, not below.

When I looked straight in the mirror, all I could ask was *Why couldn't it have been anything else?* I sat down in the empty bathtub and cried and cried. Never again. Never again. Never again. Never again.

Milk tar. Mother knocked on the door of the bathroom and asked me if she could please give me a hug. "Never again!" I shouted, and nothing could change my mind, not even something to eat or drink, not even Mother's kisses, or her crying from the bed.

miracle answer

SUGAR'S FATHER was big-muscled and short-afroed, which set all us junior high girls positively off, and the neighbor men called him "Little Oak" because he set them off in a different way. If you'd asked me, he was the youngest looking father of them all. He had been in the Marines. From our kitchen window, Mother watched him do his pushups in his driveway and she sneered. She said that even though she wasn't considered a part of our block (by the ones who made those rules, at least), *still:* she had the right to her opinions. And it's a squeaky wheel that gets the oil. And in her opinion, Little Oak Jones didn't really look like Sugar's father but like her older brother. If you had asked her. That much she could say as an outsider. But I didn't never ask her, because I hate to even think of things like that.

Sugar's father did at least sixty-five pushups in the morning, then switched over to God knows how many deep knee bends and after that military-style jumping jacks, the ones like clock hands. He lifted ten-pound weights in each arm when he went inside — I watched him in their living room window. Ten-pound weights in the afternoon and fifteen-pounders at night. I would be watching. There was so much of him, so damn lovely much! that when he did his lifting or running in place or ankle-grip stretches and when his skin glistened with that musk-man sweat of his, I could forget myself. If you'd asked me, I'd have said he was like the Masterful Man of the aftershave commercial. He smoked a clove cigarette on their front steps after his workout and filed his long lady nails. All of a sudden he would get fatherly and would warn us: Kids! That homework better be all done and be done curreckly, or I'll use some of this heren muscle! We pretend quivered.

And on the outside, even though I was just a friend invited over to do homework and in reality there wasn't no man who could order me around like that (except Mother) — on the outside, I would be like, "Yes, Mr. Jones, I'll make sure that me and Sugar and Ace get all 100s on that social studies test tomorrow!" That was on the outside. But on the inside, I would see that arm bursting right out of its sleeve in a perfect half-moon and I would be like, "Oh baby, just say the word!"

Mother would just keep on staring at Little Oak Jones as she dried the dishes. "Yep," she said, "still water runs deep. I wonder what went wrong in that family," and her voice was that sinister way that took away all my dreams and made what I saw before me look old, tired, and ugly.

Little Oak Jones usually went out around ten o'clock at night, wearing a tight turtleneck sweater and wingtips, and he usually came home round three-thirty in the morning, sometimes on his hands and knees, from where I could see. Everyone else would be sound asleep.

Another father: Mr. Jeffries. Never left his house, so he always wore bedroom slippers. When I was little, I remember him having real light, light skin, almost like Mother's, but then when I got of age, meaning old enough to start identifying fathers, I took another look and saw that Mr. Jeffries' skin was actually light brown on the verge of gray-green. A shade of grayish green. Mr. Jeffries had had spells ever since his accident and never left the house. To me, he matched the inside of their house perfectly. The armchairs with deep resting marks from old bodies, the curtains in every room that never moved, the yellow crackly plastic slipcovers on the sofas. He sat in his study, which was filled with books on airplanes and diseases and monkey-to-man stories, but they never interested us much. He would sometimes catch me and Leah as we walked past his room and then we would be in for one of his lectures: Grow Up Fine! Grow Up Fine with Manners Like Those White Kids That Didn't Need to Be Told Twice! Achieve Something in Life! Stay in School! Respect Your Elders! Protect Your Jewel! Be Chaste! Don't Hand Over Your Jewel if There Is No Bank Robbery! Know Your Roots! (Don't be ashamed of them like I was back in the old days of Curlina, worst state in the Confederacy, Lord knows we had it hard, for me there was no doubt that if you could pass, then *pass!* But we knew what suffering was back then, God why did you ever have to put black folks on this earth, the price is never finished being paid.) Always Pay Attention!

His daughter Leah was my best friend. Unlucky for her, she came out light enough for you to see when she was blushing. Her father would yell out his different lectures at us and Leah would turn the color of the dining room curtains. Me, I could see why she would hate to hear stuff like that, but I also in a way wished I was in her shoes.

Mr. Jeffries was always in his study working on his Big Project. Even Leah didn't know what it was, but she also didn't care. When we went up to her room, he asked us to "play quietly," and that made us girls giggle. For a wack old dude like that, you might a thought he was old and ugly even, but Mr. Jeffries was just the opposite. He was old, but he had just enough handsome left over on his face to make you feel sorry for him, because you knew he'd been wrecked.

We tiptoed past his study with our sandals in our hands. Leah had some magazines of naked girls, black ones and white ones, on loveseat couches, that she wanted to show me. They were in her closet. Mice couldn't have been quieter.

"Girls!" Mr. Jeffries hollered out from behind his door as we passed by. "How do you expect a man to get any serious thinking done if you all are going to be making all that racket out there? Remember, I'm the one slaving away in here so that you both don't have to endure the hardships we back in the old days had to. The bitterness — " And then he broke off and I could tell he was crying. I nudged Leah to find out what he was really talking about, but she said, "Just forget it. I got one word for that bitch: positively nuts."

Mr. Jeffries began to sob like a woman in a love story movie, so I went home, leaving Leah turning Christmas red on the stairs to her closet. I wanted to give her a hug good-bye, but she pushed me away. "Goodbye," she said, slamming the front door. I felt hurt, but for who? I couldn't say. I walked home.

Mr. Jeffries was the first father to go to bed at night. His light usually went out round 6:30 P.M.

Mother never wore makeup or very pretty dresses. The permanent had just about grown out and was just hanging on at the extra-blond ends of her hair. Her normal dresses were called "shifts" in Mays Department Store. They were full of juice stains, or blood, or rips. She would always ask, "But who do I have to dress up for?" and then look at me like I was supposed to have the answer. That made me just put my eyes to the floor and pretend like I was thinking of something else. *Who?* How the hell did I know? Mother's eyes would be staring straight at me, so blue you'd think she lay in bed at night and they glowed in the dark with that question. She did have one pretty dress, fading roses on a green background, but you really couldn't hold that against her. Because she hardly wore it then, only sometimes at night, when she was feeling that old special feeling, as if somebody else besides me loved her. She was remembering my father. It was every now and then. We put candlesticks on the table and Mother made an old favorite of ours when we were an actual family: Yankee pot roast. We would eat like we were starved.

Mr. Hill's son, Ace, was on the brink of becoming my pre-engagement boyfriend, but bad luck for him: I already knew I would hate having Mr. Hills as a father. He was a drunk who had lost all his bottom teeth, and besides that: he'd spread the rumor in our neighborhood that Mother was hot to trot, a fat-behind blonde, a hussy, a low-class slut on wheels. That she was a white woman home-wrecker out to tear the fabric of the traditional black American family. Mr. Hills had said that Mother used yellow hair color and pretty dresses to lure the family men of the block away from the safety of their homes. Sugar and Leah reported back all these items to me, so I put the romantic squeeze on Ace, telling him no more feeling my chest and stuff till he got his pops straight, but what could he do, the kid? So I went home to Mother to tell her about all this but she just laughed and shrugged her shoulders and said to me, "Oh, I thought you had something really bad to tell me." She was cool.

Me, I freaked. "Don't cry, Bea," Mother would tell me. "Remember: sticks and stones." And she'd remind me: was that the way she'd raised me? To listen to such ignorance?

She didn't care that she wasn't a part of the block — it was their loss. Couldn't I remember that? But I wasn't that strong, and I used to cry, and I would hate the fact that not only was my father gone but also the only one left for me didn't really look like me, didn't sound like me, wasn't me in a way, and that complicated matters. Why couldn't I be as strong as Mother? Sometimes I hated myself. Then other times, like when I would pretend sick and lie in bed watching cartoons and church shows on TV, I would hear Mother whimpering in the kitchen, and the words were like stars swimming in the blackest sky, little words that were almost unnoticeable, only I could hear them sliding from Mother's hurting lips: *"Where are you, Dan?"* And I would know it was not only sticks and stones.

The days usually looked like this: Mother went out in her old jeans and sweatshirts and didn't hardly talk to anybody. She swung open the back door to our station wagon, unloaded the groceries, took the lawn mower out of the garage, and started mowing the front and back. She hung up the clothes on the line in the back yard, and when somebody snoopy would pass by and pretend to say hello to her, she would wave back in real friendliness. I say pretend hello because the snoop would probably be thinking, How the hell that white girl think she could hang on to that fella? Chile or no chile, t'aint natrul.

The sun would come down behind the dying neighborhood sycamores and the sound of cooking pots would be heard all over the dimming sky. Mother watched the evening news in the kitchen after supper while I went to turn down our bed. "Are you asleep yet?" were always the first words of the night, and they would be the ones that would make us giggle and finally close our eyes. Then there was the question in Mother's eyes, the one she asked after she turned her back to me, the one that I didn't have to hear in order to hear: "Where are you, Dan?"

Above all else, I was looking for: tender, loving, caring, and caring enough to punish. Trademarks of a real father. I always believed it when fathers on television said, This hurts me more than it does you. You could always see fathers spanking the kids and loving every damn minute of it. But then there were the fathers where you had to see it in their eyes, and then you knew. You knew that this child was really a part of them, and that it really did hurt, just like if you were smacking your own face.

Mother was not the perfect father. I didn't want her to know that I thought that, because she was trying, anyone could see that, even the ones on our block. The things she said really sounded like they filled in the gap: Do your homework or else! Wash those dishes behind you! I don't care who does it, you're not everybody, and I say your hair does not need grease! I love you. Wash out that hair, please! Do that homework! Are you listening to me? Don't forget that I love you.

But did she ever punish me? The answer to that was no.

It was one of our usual fights, one that in the old days of being a family would've ended up with me getting smacked in the mouth but now it was like feathers. I told Mother I wanted to find the real me in me somewhere. After our yelling, I went over and took a good long look at my father's picture on the wall near our bathroom. I really did look like him, I thought, really the spitting image, it was just the hair that was different, just a touch different, his being a genuine afro in that picture from Independence Day at Mount Rushmore, and mine just loads of light brown frizzle that curled and did not do what I told it to and that unfortunately did not need any hair grease. Father and I had the same noses.

We had the same short eyelashes that curled into themselves. Mother loved our faces and our hands, which she said were smaller than normal. Father and I had looked so damn much alike.

And he liked to laugh and I liked to laugh. And he was good in geometry, making the sides of an isoceles triangle figure up for math problems, and I was good in short division. He could fix cars and bikes and put together radios and old TVs and he could explain to me how he fixed them (so that one day I would be able to put them back together) and I would understand him like nobody else.

He had loved to hold Mother in his arms, and so had I. He had loved to say in a whisper, "I am your rock, don't you forget it," and we had loved to hear it.

In the bathroom after the yelling I parted my hair in seven sections, sides, front, and back, and I made lines of blue grease in the spaces. The picture from Independence Day at Mount Rushmore was placed on the mirror ledge above the sink. I smelled like him: a good beginning. I teased my hair, but the afro that came out was knotty in three sections, flat and clingy in the others. *It would be much better for her and for me.* I braided one flat section of my head, but little strands kept flying out. I teased it all again so that the top of my head stood up. I pulled my fingers through it so it looked like a lawn that wasn't mowed. Mother was always saying that there was a lot of him in me. I twisted the sides of my hair down and around so that they made a crown around the parts of hair that were struggling to stay up.

Looking into the mirror above the sink, I saw the look in my father's face the night he left forever. *This hurts me more than it does you.* That night Mother had stopped cooking dinner, she'd just let the pots of rice and ham and cabbage with pepper boil over and she'd started yelling, "Go to him, go to him, just do it all the way for once!" and then there was quiet and then you could hear her foot opening and closing the garbage can over and over. I was in my bed then, planning what to do the next time my father said to me that he was planning to go away for a short spell in order to make all our lives better. I was in my bed, and I was in this state half between asleep and awake, so when Father came into my room, I didn't really know if he was there with me or still on the stairs, listening to the garbage can tell the story.

His face was like the bark of a tree in the night. Like the kind the slaves we read about in school had to feel to find their way north, to their home. His eyes were melting at me. Somewhere someone's voice said, "Sweet dreams. I can't leave you." Many hands were over me, covering me, touching my forehead and my face and my ears like a blanket of stars when you are sick in bed at night. I reached up to hug the hands but they disappeared into the air. *This hurts me.*

The door to the bathroom flashed open. Mother barked at me like a dog. She recognized the smell of the grease all the way from the hall. *"Dan,"* she barked in a wind of memory that just kept waiting for a chance to pinch her hard. She grabbed an open bottle of shampoo and let it pour over my head. "You damn savage!" she barked. *"You have gone too far!"* I cried and howled and bent my head into the sink. The water rang my head like a bell. The next thing was the sound of the shampoo bottle bouncing off my back, *thud* off the vertebrae we learned about in school! I cried hopeless tears. "You'll pay for this!" Mother hollered. "You have gone too far, and I don't want you back!" She tornadoed out, shaking the stairs on the way to the kitchen. I cried, but for who?

And downstairs, later, my dinner was waiting for me in the usual place and Mother was humming her song and folding clothes in front of the news on TV. I came down and waited. Father would've made me pay. Mother waited till after I played with my food for a while and then kissed me good-night. I felt my back ache, my vertebrae, but Mother was kind and loving to me and her voice had me in it and she never made me pay.

I couldn't decide who was the best one to fill in the blank while mine was away trying to improve me and Mother's lives. Of course, anybody I picked to stand in his place in my heart would have to promise that he would improve me and Mother's lives right here at home, and that he would never leave. He would have to punish like a father and hold our crying heads in his arms afterward and tell us that the sun would keep shining and the moon would keep staring and that he would be there for the lawn and that he was here to stay. He would have to listen to Mother's trying to fill up the empty spaces and then tell her softly that he was there to do it from now on, that now she was free, that now she could go back to being what she had been before: just a mother, now he was here. Like the faces on Mount Rushmore which told us that they were the beginning, and now all we had to do was trust.

Mr. Jeffries was in front place. I had come over to do some last-minute studying with Leah on the social studies test the next day, and Mr. Jeffries was standing in the door to his study holding a book called *They Thought They Were Free*. Leah blushed two-tone red and pink and her eyes were fiery. Her father's bathrobe had come undone and it looked like a scary forest down there. His hands were shaking. He said, "This book could've been written about *us!* What do we know? Taught in one room, seven to fifteen, no heat in the winter months, black frostbite toes, trying to make babies in the cloakroom for warmth, but we were reading books! Touching pages and letters and words. Yes sir, we were going to grow up and show North Curlina we can read and therefore we can change things. Winter into spring, mockingbirds into wasps, fields of rape into solid, brown-treed mountains. We were going to make it even without the forty acres they'd promised our grandfathers. Even without the mule! You couldn't tell us nothing! We were learning how to read. We were on the cutting edge!" And then Mr. Jeffries collapsed on the stairs leading up to Leah's bedroom and closet. He was breathing heavy and bad. Even though Leah was rolling her eyes, I suddenly felt my stomach grow ice-cold with love. I loved this man. He was being punished and he was sharing his punishment with the daughter he loved.

He looked up at us and said, "You couldn't tell us nothing. Now all you can do is laugh at us. Tell me, girls, do you think I should be laughed at?"

And Mr. Jeffries burst out crying, which suddenly made me afraid, and I didn't know if I loved him anymore, he wasn't that strong, and I turned to Leah to see what she would do. She reached down and picked her father up like he was a basket of folded laundry and she shoved him hard into his study. She slammed the door. She said, "I just can't take that bitch no goddamn more."

I said, "Oh, yeah, man, I know how you feel." Her eyes were on her feet.

She said, "He don't know what the hell he talking about. That book ain't about *us.*" She snarled in his door's direction, "He's holding up a book, talking about *us,* and you open the first page and see that it's about fucking World War Two. Give me a fucking break!"

Upstairs in her closet, Leah lit me and her a cigarette to

share. I was wondering if Mr. Jeffries would come a little bit more to earth if he had me — a normal girl who had learned something about the way to treat a father. If he would have Mother to steady him. I watched Leah puff and hiss. She was not the kind of child who would ever feel more hurt than the father did.

Mr. Jeffries hollered from his study, "I hope you girls aren't smoking up there!" and then he slammed a few doors. I breathed. He was more with us now.

Leah lit one cigarette after another. In the dark, I could tell that she was looking at me, waiting for something, like I was supposed to have it. But I didn't have it.

She turned away from me. Later she told me something new. Leah had just slept with a boy and now she was scared. I waited a few minutes, and I put my arms around her. Now she was like my sister. At first she was quiet, just puffing and hissing her cigarette away. Then she said, "Just who the hell thinks he is free? Give me a fucking break!" and her almost white face melted into a lake of frantic steady tears.

Little Oak Jones went out of the question. Mother watched his pushups and sneered and didn't find him in the least bit sexy. She looked at him and did not see the Masterful Man. She shook her head in laughter and just went back to drying the dishes like it wasn't a fantastically handsome father-and-husband specimen out there doing his thing but a corny dude out to impress junior high girls. I made the move that had been on my mind.

I said, "Mother, maybe we should invite Sugar and her father over for some dinner sometime maybe and see how we all get along if we like each other maybe more than neighbors like a family maybe." Mother looked up and waited a minute and let out a horse laugh. "Beatrice," she said, "Beatrice, baby." Then she broke into that sinister look, the one I hated so much, only this time she didn't laugh. She said, "Besides, something is just not right over there. Looks like there's a mystery in that family, if you ask me." I went out of the kitchen and turned my mind off like a TV.

One of the great things that I forgot to mention was that my father, before he left to improve our lives, allowed me to have Ace Hills as a boyfriend. Mother ranted and swore that if I was ever up to something with Ace, she'd ground me. And she would hold up the pepper mill that we kept on the kitchen table as a sign of things that might come. Because Mother was young once too and hindsight is 20-20. The early bird catches the worm.

Father took me into the living room where he would have had a man-to-man talk with me if I had been a son. He asked me if I was serious about Ace. I said I didn't know. I said I thought it was time I had a boyfriend, I was going on thirteen. Father said, You won't let him get to your head, will you? I smiled no, because I knew that that was the answer, that was the answer he wanted to hear, that was the truth in my heart. He knew he didn't have to worry. He could depend on me. I could depend on me.

Where are you, Dan?

Mother headed me off at the pass. She held the front door open as I walked in from school. In the background, Sugar's father was deep-kneeing against his Cadillac convertible. The sun was coming down early. The leaves were all over.

She introduced us: "Beatrice, Wilhelm. Wilhelm, my baby, Beatrice." I nodded at the white man holding a bouquet of baby roses. We didn't have to say any words. His hair was like golden straw in fairy tales. He had soft blue eyes and what looked like a heart full of warm-oven love. He took my hand in his. It started with my head, then my back. I cracked all over.

Fire engines couldn't have been louder. One, two, three, bang, boom. Ace was managing to get in there occasionally and separate them. I was like the woman in the disaster movie who cries even before she knows there is no hope whatsoever — her tears still have a little prayer of a chance in them. Leah sat like a prizefighter on one corner of her bed in her room and I embraced her as I screamed, "This is not how it's supposed to be!"

She breathed in deeply. Her hair was glistening with hot sweat and relaxer and was pasted on her from her forehead down to her neck. Then she would look up and see him, see Nelson, a boy I once had a crush on, Sugar's older brother, almost out of the eleventh grade, now maybe the father, and she would rush over at him and try to scratch his eyes out like a cat. "I hate your stinking guts! I wish I could shoot your stinking ass!" she screamed. Nelson said, "Don't turn me away, baby, I want to be there for you, I want to be there for you and our son, you my life, you all I have to live for," and he said it like it was a song from Billboard's Top Twenty. Leah said, "I have your fucking seed in me. I'm going to be sick big-time!" Nelson said back, "Don't deny me the chance to love you the way it should be done." Ace got in the middle and pulled Leah off Nelson. She had cut two deep marks into his cheek. I cried because my heart was broken. Downstairs, Mr. Jeffries was silent. It was the first time.

Mother was crying. "Couldn't you at least try to look at him as your new father?" she asked me. Her head was in the sofa cushion.

I said, "He's nowhere near the thing we need here, Mother." My voice was low, and it was trying to sting her.

She cried, "I'm lonely." Then she whispered, "I'm lonely, Beatrice. And he makes me unlonely. He fills in my blank. He takes me back to where I come from."

I said, "But you are here, and this is where you have to stay. You can't leave too!"

Mother said, "I could have someone if only you let me. He could always be here for me. I could talk German again. I could love him and laugh in these faces on this block. I could sleep and I could laugh just at the air if I felt like it. Most of all, I could love you better as your mother."

I said, "He won't understand me. He will hate me. He will hate this block. He won't understand us. And then he will leave. Simple as that."

Mother laughed. I was expecting her to comfort me with her blanket of love words, it was time for the miracle answer, only this time I was waiting for it, but instead she pulled me over to her in a hug and said, "Why was I blessed with such a selfish daughter?" I buried my head in the other cushion.

Mother said, "I'm not that old, Bea. He's a man I could start a new family with. Wouldn't you like that?"

And her voice was pretty with the future in it and hopeful and lovely, and it closed on my heart like a granite window.

Leah was calmer. Ace had taken Nelson down to where the bathroom was. I used to have a crush on him, Nelson. When I was liking him, I never knew that he had a father in him. And he wasn't that bad-looking after all. I wished Leah knew how lucky she really was.

Seeing her on her bed like that, I thought there were many things I wanted to tell her. Like, why don't we shape up her father and plug him in with my mother? Like, why do things turn out so strange, especially when you have such a brilliant master memory? There were people who spent their whole lives going along with you, pretending to help you along the way, not stepping on your toes, then the end to that comes as fast as a ray of sun. They turn around, these supposed people on your side, and they make your life miserable. They do the damage, then leave. They smile at you and they don't realize that all the time their smile is cracking you in two.

Here Leah had a boy who wanted to be a good father. He wanted to be a father, for Christ's sakes alive! He wasn't like the other boys in eleventh grade, who just wanted the trophy. And he was good-looking. I used to want him, but I let him go when Ace wanted me. He was Sugar's older brother, son of the Masterful Man, but he didn't look like any of them. Why didn't Leah see she'd been blessed?

She rubbed her hands on her light brown belly. She was fourteen and still in the seventh grade. She said, "I'm not going to let him trap me." Then she walked over to me and kissed me gently on my forehead. She said, "What if it was just you and me?" Then she kissed me gently on the lips. Maybe her tongue touched me a little, I don't remember, but I didn't *not* like it. Then she went downstairs to throw Nelson out. There was some more crying, Nelson didn't want to leave. Mr. Jeffries came out of his room and tossed Nelson out the door like a bag. Leah fainted in Ace's arms. Mr. Jeffries began to slam his head into the door over and over till it was a little bloody. Everywhere you looked there was hurting.

Mother made us go to the movies as a family. What made it worse was that we walked all the way to the theater. What made it *the worst* was the way Mother was walking: happy, almost skipping, like a lot of years in her life had never happened, like this was the start she'd dreamed of as a girl.

The movie we saw was *Evergreen*. While we were watching it, Wilhelm reached down to my ear and asked me if I would be his friend. I shrugged. When the lights came on, he put his arm around me.

On the way home, the block stopped and stared. Old ladies waved hello to my mother and smiled at her in the dearest way they'd ever done. Mrs. Hills said, "What a lovely couple!" behind our backs as we passed. It made Mother smile a stone anchor that took me down.

Wilhelm said to me, "I'll treat you like you are my own."

I thought Oh God no, Oh God no, Oh God no, Oh God no to the beat of my steps all the way home till I finally said it out loud enough for him to hear and he just smiled at me.

Mr. Jeffries held up a notebook and threw it at me and Leah. It could've hit her belly, but I don't think he knew that. It was his Big Project. I loved him suddenly. He was going to tell us about it. Leah's eyes were red and bloody-looking.

He said, "This here is what I am working my life away at, try thinking about that the next time you are fucking." Leah passed out. Ace picked her up from his feet. I kept on listening.

Mr. Jeffries said, picking up the notebook, "This is the book that would've saved you, girl. Would've taken you off this small-head block and sent you to the best university, to the government of this here country. It was all in this book. The way I was going to make you make the most of yourself."

He said, "Do you want to know what this book is about? Do you care?"

Leah kept her eyes closed.

He continued, "It is about the never-ending fight for our identity, the quest to know ourselves in spite of them telling us who we are. It is about a boy growing up in Curlina who gets to leave it and who then gets caught up in political things that confuse his mind and who then gets swallowed up by *them*. It's a story that's been on my mind for a long time. It's a story that will make lots of us recognize ourselves and then change. Work for change."

Another thing I didn't mention was that Leah loved to read, and when her father went on about this book, she woke up and listened and burst out laughing, "My father, lock him up in a prison all day long and he can't even write a shitty book straight! Hey, old man, ain't you ever read *The Invisible Man?*" She was doubled over. She said to me, "Beatrice, things can't get no worser." Later on, after she had cursed her father out and made him fall down on the bed in his room, she told me, "I think things are going to go uphill from here." She stopped laughing and started grinning.

Me, I watched Mr. Jeffries' puzzled look, like someone had just switched on the lights, and I wanted him in my life more than ever. Mr. Jeffries, I was saying in my mind, we were both fooled.

He flipped back and forth through the pages. Leah and Ace went into the kitchen to make dinner. Leah was saying, "You know, Ace, I think I will name my baby Lee, after me. And you know, I think I'll love this kid after all. I might just have another one right after this one. But you think I'ma let that funky Nelson on me, you dead wrong. Me, I got my eyes on Little Oak. I'm going to really let him check my homework. Ha-ha!" Ace put his arm around Leah's shoulder. Mr. Jeffries mumbled to himself, staring into nothing. I felt like saying, "You'll always have a daughter in me," but I didn't. Because Mr. Jeffries wasn't waiting for anything from me.

It had actually been Mother's idea to visit Mount Rushmore. Father and I had wanted to go to Carlsbad Caverns, but Mother said it would be especially good for me to learn about our Founding Fathers. Father agreed. In those days, he always agreed. The heads of Mount Rushmore stared us straight in the face. The warm air made us take off our shoes and laugh at the other tourists. *They weren't us.* Father told Mother and me that he was glad we'd come, that this was a bit of history every man should absorb before his time comes. All the time he was talking, Mother had tears in her eyes. He looked over and said, "See that one there, Thomas Jefferson?"

Then he said, "That man was in love with a slave at his home. He loved her in spite of not being able to. He didn't give her her freedom when it counted, but they loved each other in a way that they chose to make secret for the rest of history." He stepped back and gazed. He had love and hate in his eyes, on and off, far and near.

I said, "But it ain't a secret, Father. You know about it."

He said, "But it was a secret. For them then and for us now. Things like that weren't supposed to be, and now — " And Mother cut him off and asked him why spoil a perfect day? Let's just think of the good things and put bad history behind us. We can only go on from here. And I agreed with Mother and I hugged her back when she reached out to me. It couldn't get any better, my blood was telling me in my body. Father kissed us both on the head. The faces of Mount Rushmore looked down. I looked back. Mother and Father started walking back to the other tourists.

"Aren't you going to come with us?" Father yelled when I stood there with the four stone heads. "Of course." I laughed.

inside, a fountain

MY GRANDMOTHER was telling me about the chair her husband had made for her before the war. I was supposed to be impressed. I felt my black braid extensions glisten all in her face. I was supposed to learn and appreciate my good blood and make some stupid remark like yes I know good blood is good. At that moment, I had the applesauce bowl in my hand, ready to feed her so she could take the pill down easier, and up on the telling at that moment, it was the one about the chair when there was nothing else to be had in the entire land. What had separated them from the others. She would say, Imagine that! *Give me a break.*

My grandmother always had to be fed, on account of special kidney pills or heart condition or general nerves. Every hour, make sure you dunk a pear or a piece of bread or a slice of liverwurst or some thickened milk down her throat. A piece of rum cake. No alcohol, being that diabetes is another affliction, but hell we're just talking one piece of cake. A spoon of fruit salad with yogurt. A pork chop. She will smile and chomp away like a fool and in the middle of it all will be these stories. Yesterday she was the Prisoner for Allied Sex. Today, the Chair in the War. And tomorrow, Her Mother

Who Died the Day after the Germans Surrendered. The blood, the blood. The lines. Shame. She looks at me and frowns. She realizes that something stopped. It stopped with what is sitting right in front of her. There's blood, and there's me. I'm looking right back at her. Germany once was the Big Blood. But keep this in mind, old lady: I'm doing destiny now.

I was in Germany, getting dinner ready for my granny and her rough nephew Josef who was my mother's cousin and friend, and trying to think up the right kind of insult to lay on my own distantly related cousin or something, Danya. The kind of insult that would get results. Not just crying as results, but finally comprehended *knowledge*. The perfect way for me to indicate to her, *You may be something* here, *but in Newport News you wouldn't be nothing. And furthermore, I'm going to be staying. I am part of the past. This house has a stable with real horses in it and a Mercedes out front. They are mines. There is a room where I keep my things in a dresser that has my smell all over it inside. It is mines. There are people in this place that look like my mother. I look like my mother. I'm here to stay.*

But none of that was a really good insult. None of that would take her anywhere. Her mind would not comprehend. I needed to get my point across.

Here I was in Germany, doing the same old same old thing: helping get dinner ready. Just like when I was a girl on the verge of womanness in Newport News, helping to get dinner ready, only here I was in Germany, a little later. In addition to that: sweeping the floor, mopping the hall, shining the silverware, cleaning the spots my grandmother left behind whenever she got up, eating my food, getting in the car, going every Sunday with everybody to the Viking cemetery for potfuls of old pride, looking at the muddy hills and trying to recall the greatness, sleeping in the bed, seeing him, my Virginian, the navy man in my dreams, asking him why not now? Why not? Keeping an eye on this girl who is my cousin by blood no matter what, watching her, feeling sorry for everything, wishing that there really was something like going backward in time, dusting the tables, scrubbing the horses' backs, looking my mother's cousin Josef up and down when the chance presented itself, taking him in because he might finally change his mind about me one of these days and say to me for the rest of the world to hear, "Your Search Has Ended."

The kitchen here is the kind where people are forced to talk to each other because it is big with ceilings and not warm. You walk around flapping your arms against your chest like a duck. In Germany people say that blacks are used to that hot heat from their home, that place they came from, and at this point I always have to say, "You mean Newport News, Virginia?" and they think that means I have a terrific sense of humor. They need to point out to me, No, Africa, the original place. They need to point things out to me.

The oven gives off streams of smoke. In the kitchen things are black all around. Danya, my relative, fakely innocent, says to me as I just sit there with my head on the table, "Come and peel potatoes with me from dinner, my dears." It's supposed to be *for* and not *from*, but we each know where the other is coming from. Danya has this juicy smile. If she were back in Newport News, she could easily go for twenty, twenty-seven. She is into hiding her goods. She waits. She waits for the best ambush moment. Then she says, "What is you looking so happy for, Cousin Florence?"

Another mistake sentence. Mistake sentences can get you love. Danya is big on getting all the love she can. In reality I know that she is proud she can make sentences after being just six months in English class in the tenth grade. And most of her sentences are correct ones, like: *How do you do? How does your family fare? From which part of the country do your people hail?* Most of them are right on target and indicate, as they say, the wide horizons of the brain.

Because they teach them differently here in Germany than they do American kids in America. I myself don't know any kid back home, especially the ones at Booker T. Washington High in Newport News, that could learn anything in six months like these kids. We all had to learn our subjects good and all, but we were what you would call slow, and we got left back a lot of times, and anyway we were not proud of most of our subjects the way the teachers kept telling us we should be.

Because tell me, who would be proud of learning something like for instance: your family once had been kidnapped by a slave ship sauntering across the ocean, being that they had one time been called "the finest specimens of the current crop." They jumped overboard into nowhere when the shipmen sexed them up in broad daylight on the decks and the captains laughed and hollered, "Welcome to your New World. Heh." Who the hell would be proud?

And to top that off, we learned sentences like: *Although they suffered for a time, they demonstrated the human endurance and inherent Christian perseverance evident in their beings to know that they must wait for the hands on the clock of destiny to turn. Look at the souls who blessed this earth only because others had stayed on board: Harriet Tubman, Mammy, George Washington Carver, our own Booker T. You are part of them. This is what is known as heritage, because of the ones that stayed, because of the ones who concealed a being greater than the slavish exterior would permit to be guessed.* Who would be proud?

Danya kept looking at me, stripping the helpless skins off the potatoes. She was waiting for an answer. I washed my hands. I dried them in the cloth. Her English mistakes sparked off one of those moments when the tears made my chin shake and got me thinking of the grisly way blood can work.

And then there was this new man to think about, my mother's rough cousin. Josef. He was the place where I was living in Germany. The only one in the family that would give my mother the time of day. Josef. His face was old. He looked young in the body, but his face had leftover teenage acne and old hurt in it that came from not forgiving. He walked into the kitchen. He didn't look at me. His hands were muddy from the horses, which he had to clean all alone now that Katinka, the girl in the stables, had walked out and left him flat. She did it the same way as in the movies. She held her head high and finished buttoning her blouse up to the chin. She brushed her hands together as if Josef were lint. The back of her head told him: I'm on to you. When she walked out, Josef gave me a look, me shoveling hay in the corner stall for those damn horses, and then he told me to go take care of my granny, because what did I think it was, a vacation? She was not a vacation, in case that's not already clear as day.

I was moved into the kitchen, partial food detail for my old grandmother. My mother's mother. I couldn't stand Danya and she could not stand me and often my mother's cousin made like he hated my everlasting guts. I swore to love him no matter. So we all went along in that kind of circle.

Over the stove there was this picture of my mother when she was a girl here in Germany. It was her and her horse framed in silver. It was a funny thing. The picture said, "First Place Young Women Equestrians of Hamburg 1959." I knew that that was how my mother had got out of shoveling out the old hay and sweeping the shit away in the stable in the old days. That was the path you had to escape down if you didn't want to lead a regular horse life and drown. That was the path that required thinking. My mother was always good at that: thinking ahead.

Another story my grandmother loved to tell us besides the chair was the Allied occupation. This made her blush. Their house had been the biggest in town. The best kitchen. The nicest horses in the stalls. The British came in and thought about smashing all their shit, but then they decided just to stay there. My grandmother and her kids, the whole mess of them, forced down into a hole in the ground, to live. Every few hours up for air. Sometimes she had to do things. At first she begged for mercy. They told her she would learn to like it. Now she couldn't remember what it was that was so bad. Our house was chosen by the enemy, she says, because we were the best.

Josef stood at the kitchen door with his hands on his hips like a woman and asked, "So who's going to feed the grandmother tonight?" He was staring at the famous picture of my mother.

Danya as usual said, "Well, if it's me again." She was chopping the red cabbage into rows like the army. She liked to be the unlikely candidate.

This time I jumped into the act. Eight months waiting period is over, you suckers. Let *me* at my grandmother. I said, "Let me have a try. She belongs to me too." Eight months is over tonight. Their faces went right into panic overdrive. They were thinking that she was having those nightmares because of me, the ones where no one could sleep afterward. A lie. For me, this was the start.

He laughed mysteriously. "So you think you can take care

of your grandmother?" Then he said, "As if she didn't already have a mountain of worries in her soul already." He snorted a few times. He was putting up his usual fight.

I said, "Look, I been cooking and cleaning more than you know. *Everything* is more than you know. I want to help my grandmother eat. Why is there any harm in that? There ain't no real harm in that."

Josef said, "Grmph."

I said, "Everything is more than you know."

Danya looked over his way and then she closed her eyes and shrugged her shoulders. She said she didn't care. Then she said, "Just be careful you don't do nothing crazy, like poison her by accident or nothing. Oh you know me, I just joking." The girl was into hiding her goods.

My mother's cousin said "Grmph" again. You would think in eight months I would get accustomed, but every time it was like a knife. I reached into the cabinet for the special plate and special fork. I grabbed my grandmother's special cup out of its hiding place in the corner and I said, "Now I got you!"

What I usually said when it got to who was going to feed my old granny was "What you thinking, I'ma kill her or something?" but then it wouldn't go no further. Josef would look in my eyes for a long time and then he would shift to my hair, a good place to take me down. My hair is different. It's like the horses' hair. My hair is pitch black, and the braids hang down my back in no pretty way. It's tough. I can't get any relaxer here in Germany. So everything on me just stands still and prays for time to move on.

Also my arms. My mother's cousin would look at my arms. They were too strong and meaty to be a girl's. He called them "working limbs," and that of course was another one of those things you could take as a joke. He said it was due to the fact that I must have been a slave girl at home, and still he went and started laughing all hysterical when he finished calling them "working limbs." And plus: I was what Bann's Department Store in Newport News would call a full-figured gal. I was roomy.

I wasn't allowed to feed my grandmother. They said that even though she was crazy, there was the shock to think of. An unpretty black girl in a house in Germany. All they would say was that I brought back some old days. But I would be realizing, mostly there was the shock.

A German girl smells like Koelnisch Wasser. A German girl has that light ancient scent to her and is always sparkling. A German girl knows when to stop and when to let out the whisper, "I like the way of *that* caress." A German girl is smart and handsome, a word you wouldn't normally use for girls in Newport News. A German girl wakes up to a window in the bright morning and lets the sun pat her face warm into the world.

A German girl can speak many languages. She is adept at the language of the inside and the language of the outside. "Me? I can master the language of love. I am as light as the forsythia in spring, as a waterfall bubbling somewhere in the mountains, all the treasures that everyone sees in me. What about you?"

It's one of those times when Danya has me frightened to look in the mirror when I'm by myself, or to think about myself, the way I am in reality. Just look at me.

Five-foot-five, a hundred seventy-four pounds. Caring warm individual that doesn't take a whole lot to satisfy. Is willing to learn. Don't want to be left by the wayside. Brown skin. *Dark* brown skin. Gray eyes. Nothing much from the mother, who is light and ash-blond and curled, soft, slippery. Nothing, but still a joy. Can cook, can tend a house good, can do most anything. Knows the way to most hearts. Loved a *man* for the first boyfriend in her life. Wants to discover about life. Never wants to be on a boat, of any kind. Learned a lot from the navy, and other sources. Learned, for instance, it is possible to hold yourself in your arms and be intense. Nothing much from the outside, although has occasionally been told otherwise. Inside, a fountain.

I walked over to tell my grandmother that dinner was on the way. She was mountainous, white hair and spotty arms and a small, sometimes joyful face. It wasn't as if I never had the opportunity to go through most of these motions before. There were those dinnertimes after the horse shows, and then all those days in the winter when it used to be Katinka's job, only she hated to be around old people and so she burned the food and smartly got out of that duty. That was when she had first started being our girl. Katinka had said she wanted to be in the stables near my mother's cousin Josef. Her hair was red and she had slim ready arms and what you would call an attractive walk. You noticed her and kept that notice in your heart. My job in those days was that I had to call the people when the food I had just cooked was ready. This after a whole day of not doing much else but sitting on my bed and trying to read the TV guide for Germany. Or the knitting magazines for busy women.

Danya came to live with us. Her mother had said, "This is just an experiment. Just for a little while," but when it came time for Danya's version, she said, "This is just a vacation."

My grandmother was sitting in the hallway by the dining room in her special chair. She was always trucking back to the old days. You never knew what to expect. The chair smelled of wood and quilting and pee. When it was to the point that you had to hold your breath, you knew that she had gone back to the Second War times. That was when her husband went and slept with all the girl fugitives, runaways. Or sometimes she went back to the day my father spread himself out in front of her truck, or the time when the American military police told them as a joke that they were going to lynch my grandfather, or the afternoon my mother pissed at the dinner table. She had said, "If you say one more thing against it, I'll go right ahead. Just try and see if I don't go right on ahead." My grandmother was an expert in remembering those kinds of stories.

I told her, "*Grossmutter*, it's soon time for me to help you eat soon." Those were little words in English that I could get by her. She nodded at me. There is a whole lot you can see in her face, but don't linger too long. Horses, blood, children, quilts with holes, fields, rainy nights, waterfalls, police stations, gasoline cans, dead flowerbeds, potatoes, matches, stones and rocks. I never lingered too long by her face. I could feel her hands, though. They were like spiderwebs out in the rain that had that cool watery slip to them, like feathers. She liked it that I took her hand in mine. And that I was staring right into it, like a gypsy. I was looking for the answer, and maybe she knew what it was, because then she would wake up from wherever she was in her mind and grin. We used to sit like that together. Sometimes there wouldn't hardly be any light on near us, and it was just the creaky sounds of the house that floated up through the floor and touched our bellies. And pinned us together. Like a husband and a wife.

The thing that heated everyone up around here was that when they saw me, they couldn't help but see my grandmother. A whole line. It made them upset as hell, but like my mother said, God didn't take out the time to ask any of us what our choice was.

My grandmother held me in her hand. She nodded to a definite beat. I felt it too. That house was talking to us, telling tales. I could hear it, and other things, rise from the floor and into our feet.

God didn't take out the time. Because if you're talking about choices now, you must know that this wasn't mine. They propped up the fact that there were horses here and that there was a real live Mercedes here in the garage next to the stable and that this family used to have butlers and girls. But still, even in the face of those props, I can close my eyes right in their faces and say: Seventeen years all on Century Road. You don't pass that way every day.

The Speedy Quick Store, the Captain Fried Chicken with the drive-through window, Dave's Worship Car Wash, the Century Laundrymat. A little farther up and you get to the houses where the creek stench hits. All the pretty flower-beds around there and the sweet-smelling trees and little statues stooping on everybody's lawns — just a setup. The creek stench was the thing you couldn't escape. They'll never be able to sell those houses again, not in a million years, property value shot to hell, my mother always informed me.

Then comes the junction of Century and Mercury Boulevard, at the United Way building, where you will find one room with slow kids getting help with their reading and in the next room a table with slow grown-ups doing the self-same thing. Then there's the office where little boys get men to take them out on dates, like having a day at the beach or at King's Dominion or other assorted fun. It's just to give the mother who doesn't have a steady husband a break once in a while. Things like that.

It's a building we always drove past on our way to other places: Food Lion, Booker T. Washington parent-teacher conferences, Lumber Village, Second Time Around clothes store, Century Seed. We went everywhere together. I was always trying to figure out ways to do things for my mother, like writing out the grocery list with prices already put down next to the items or looking out from the car window to spot possible traffic tie-ups or accidents that might cause us a delay. My mother never drove by that United Way building without rolling her eyes and saying, "Jesus, I wish someone would give me a goddamn break."

Follow Mercury a ways, then you get to the best beach in the world. Especially if you go at night. The navy boats would be out there on the water. They would have lights winking at you from the other side of the bay. They promised you something. They promised you something good. Crabs wiggled out of the sand at night and they would want to squeeze you. If you were a girl, you had to hold somebody tight. If you were a girl, you noticed that the lights inside your own body had started winking, and you felt like showing it.

Our house was back at the beginning of Century Road. A skip and a jump from Captain's Fried Chicken. A long walk from where the creek stench hits. There was a little garden out back where my mother planted butter beans and carpet roses and Holland tomatoes. There was a little doghouse that only had a wasps' nest in it. There was a patch of peppermint weeds you could dry in the oven and then boil up. My mother had a room that was connected to mine by the bathroom. All the tiles underneath the tub had slant cracks in them. They felt cold to the touch and they all had different names: Carla, Tonya, Vionna, Sister. They were mine. They spoke a secret language to me.

Anytime, anyplace, with my eyes closed and my head shut down, I can touch the wood floor of our kitchen with my feet. It isn't cold. It is toasty, the kind only in dreams. The nails aren't hit in all the way and the shapes in the wood grain look like ghosts. The calmest place on earth for peace. No need to leave it. My smell was everywhere. Now don't even talk to me about choices, because if you do . . .

And there was also that Sunday when I first got here in Germany, when all of us took a drive up to the Viking cemetery. This was where the ancestors lived. A ship town, like Newport News. My grandmother was in the car but she kept telling us to raise a white flag before we went any farther. Later on Danya discovered that she had taken her special plate and cup in the car and then later on we all felt around to see where she'd done wet the seat. Grandmother said, "It's every man for himself." Katinka was with us, but in the front seat, and at that she rolled her eyes, which were green and slanted, and said in German something like "I'll be damned if you get me to call her 'Ma.'" To that effect.

The cemetery was a bunch of green-and-gray hills. There was tradition everywhere you looked, Josef told us, and didn't that just make you want to burst with pride. Our family could be traced back to one of these hills. Our family going back to the Vikings. Proud warriors and discoverers. You could smell the pride. It was on the trees on the hills, on the birches, the weeping willows. The weather was the same, pride rain. My mother's cousin got out and stood off by himself, looking out on a hill and the sun just happened to be going down. Danya told me that he had tears in his eyes. Later he came over and said to us in a evil whisper, "Don't you women feel anything?" Katinka put her arm around his shoulders. It was the only time Danya and I were bunched together. We were cousins; there was no way you could deny that right then.

The hills were soggy and smudged. The fog was dragging on in. Suddenly there were some teen boys standing at another hill, giving Danya the eye. My grandmother, who had made her way out of the Mercedes, started crying, "Let's dig her up! I know she's in here somewhere." It was pitiful, where the ancestors lived. After that my grandmother fainted, and when she got up, she said she couldn't walk or nothing. We all had to carry her back to the car. Josef gave me that look, without my breathing a word. The heat was everywhere. It was blasting us at every turn. We all stood around the car, away from the moss mudhills. We all tried to feel the right thing: I'm special and there is something that can prove it. Nobody could really move. A hill garden of heartbreak with a live Mercedes in it.

Look at me. It's like a piece that's trying to fit in the right spot of the puzzle. Say there are five hundred pieces. Say there is only one you. The easiest thing to do is curl up in a ball at night and wonder why. Why did she give you up? Why was he gone away? Why ain't God give us choices? It's like a big plug into a little hole. Just stay in that ball. Don't let them in on your thinking. It's just a black ball made of threads of days, days, years.

Because back in the day, in Newport News, my mother had said to me, "You ain't doing this for the second time in my family. No, ma'am. You going to get going. Don't talk to me about old love. The well's done dry up. You going to show them and all the world. You are a *fountain*. A *fountain* that ain't winding up where I did so they can turn round and say, 'A second damn time.' And they will all be laughing. *No*, *ma'am.*" And she hit me on my back with a brush. All the crying in the world was useless. Somehow my lip got busted. My insides felt delivered up in a million shreds. Then she started in with her belt.

My grandmother's special fork was really a spoon with little teeth at the end. The special cup was a baby one that had a pointy plastic nipple up top for safety. Things didn't spill so fast. But if they ever did, my mother's cousin Josef was sure to blow his stack. He hated seeing old people dribble and then act like it was something they had total control over, like something that they could've prevented. He would slam his hand down on the table and somebody's dish would rattle. My grandmother would say, "I lived to make you happy. Why don't you just take me out back and set me on fire?" and then she would burst into tears. Or she would recollect the time she managed to find that body in the Viking cemetery and save it from being lost forever. Or she would let him know that she had worked all her life just to see her family all grow into something good, something that she could see her own self in, something that would recall not only her mother the teacher in Berlin but her grandmother the artist who had painted the monarchs or her uncle who had been decorated for all those fantastic deeds of heroism during the war. One of those famous wars. Josef would just growl. He would say something that I wouldn't get, because there was so much I wouldn't get, being that they really didn't want me to bother and learn the curse words too good.

My grandmother's special plate was a plate with three compartments, like a TV dinner. That always returned her to joy. That made her shine like she must have before, in the old days. She held on to her plate with both her hands while Danya loaded up all three holes. Potato pancakes and asparagus and thick bacon. Or cucumber salad and fried apples and beef strips. Or boiled potatoes in two holes and a sunnyside egg. The list could go on.

My mother, you could see her in my grandmother's face. Or look at the hands. Cool slip like a feather. A whole line.

Danya stared at me like a slow evil dog while I helped my grandmother into her place at the table. Josef had said no dinner for him, he needed to get some things straight with the stable girl. He would be back later. He was wearing a shirt and a bow tie that was for church, which by the way we never went to. My grandmother looked my way for a long time and then she asked me, "Do I know you?" In the background you could hear Danya whining, "See all the agony you cause her?"

I turned to fill up her special plate with cabbage, potato pancake, and pork. Tomorrow I would spoon her fried eggs, fried potatoes, spinach. It was going to stay like this.

I put my grandmother's hand on the special fork. I held it tight. Together, we are going to lift this to your mouth. See that girl right there, the one who's been doing this all along? Well, now it's me. It's gonna be me. How do you like the way that food tastes now? How about in exchange for me helping you out like this, you teach me some more of that language you speak.

You know, the language of love.

My mother was laughing. I didn't understand it. In April she got these hysterical laughing fits and shit, but I didn't want to linger there too long. Then two months passed. And it was really hot. Those two months were the longest I had ever known. Two long hot musty months. She kept laughing. I kept my eyes rolled up to heaven. No messing with me and destiny. End-of-the-school-year heat blast: temperature a hundred degrees and counting. I was graduating. I was up there with Mailika and Tasha and company and I could see the brown navy head that was my future husband hiding up underneath the bleachers outside, where my mother was sitting, all proud and shit. We could stop sneaking around. We could proclaim our undying passion to the earth. No messing with what eternity has determined to be your fate.

At graduation I got a special diploma for excellent attendance. Life was my clam. I had bought the Sure Woman test and now it was safe underneath the bathroom sink, with the cleaners and toilet snake, waiting for me to get home and see what lights the future would hold.

Later at home, I checked and there was no baby inside me. So this was what destiny was telling me. I called him up and he said, "Let's keep on trying, honey, you know you got it in you." He was a grown man and knew things. I had a grown man.

Four and a half days later, the heat hit. I was as unsuspecting as the day is long. I come in from hanging with Tasha and Mailika and there is my mother going through my dresser, pulling out all my things. She has the plane ticket in her hand. She don't explain a thing. All she does is pack my things. Then she starts talking about my father, who we do not talk about. I cry. We do not talk about him. He tried to set my grandmother's house on fire. He got courtmartialed. Then he married her daughter.

There's a safe place for me in Germany with her old folks who really can't stand the sight of her but will at least give me a future. You think you know the meaning of destiny? Well, I'll tell you: your butt is not going to do this for a second time. Your butt is not getting messed up over some man. Your butt's gonna get the right one. The right kind. I'll tell you, I'm doing destiny now.

And there was her cousin Josef meeting me at the airport in Hamburg. He said, "Crying don't get you nowhere. You got your life in front of you." Then at the house, after we had finished driving there in the Mercedes and he showed me the horses, he said, "I have a girl helping out with the horses. You can help her. You can get to know her. I think she'll be more like family soon enough." He was proud. I was probably the first person he thought would believe him.

And then standing there in the driveway was my old grandmother. Old as a ripe peach on the verge. She looked my way and said, "I got dressed because you was coming. You was coming," and Josef said low, "This is her daughter. This is the most you're going to get." And me, at first I felt them tears coming on again, but then I was feeling proud because I reminded myself that there was a bit of the language I could get. That, and the fact that someone back home was thinking of me, waiting for me to escape. I stopped my tears. Either that or he was going to be coming for me soon. My navy man. God was my witness.

One of the last scenes to the old days was when I was packing my suitcase. My head was buzzing. And didn't anything make any sense. I had been so careful. That Sure Woman test had been hidden so well. After I took it from under the sink, it went into the wasp doghouse. I kept asking myself *How?* into the suitcase, and didn't anything make any sense.

I was almost finished packing my things when my mother got to hunting me down on the lawn, trying to teach my back some sense with the garden hose. She belted hard. I was screaming, "What about the neighbors? It was just my graduation day the other day!" and I knew it didn't make any kind of sense but it was one of those moments when all the loose ends came out and you realized the dead fact that your mouth was really too small to allow the sentences to break out proper that belonged together. And there was that heat, burning you up, burning that tongue, making your mouth and your head smaller and tinier and tinier and that Sure Woman test was hid so good it must have been the bathroom tiles that told her, yes the bathroom tiles ratted on you yes the shit-filled bathroom tiles didn't want to share you with anyone else yes it was them damn bathroom tiles Carla Tonya Vionna Sister yes it was you yes it sure as a woman sure as hell was you.

My mother was telling me at the airport just how lucky I was. To get to know my German side and go and find a good university and be somebody. To get to know young men, as much as possible, who had a positive future in front of them. Not any deadbeats. She said, "And my sister might probably send her little girl on over there to keep you company, the sister who don't speak to me no more, but if it's for my little girl?" Perhaps nobody would refuse me anything. Now stop that crying. Think of all the love I'll have the opportunity to get my hands on.

Now. My grandmother was at the table smelling me. Dinner was still on the table. She breathed in around my hair, then her nose pressed on my arm. She took it in. She breathed me all in. A smile was spreading. It was a smile of remembering, anyone could have told you that. Her nose slid down to my elbow crack. The fingers on one hand went up to my neck and started dancing there, making little circles, ones I almost could not feel. She breathed in my chest. She touched my face with her hand. It was all this breathing. It was slow but it moved.

From the other side of the table, Danya said, "This disgust me. You think you're going to get anywhere by that?" Then she added a few seconds later, "You adding her agony." Danya bent over and whispered something in my grandmother's ear, but that didn't make her stop breathing me in. The insult in me just laughed but didn't feel the need to budge out my mouth.

And then, later on in the hallway, the first word me and my grandmother practiced together was *Kriegszeit.* Translated: wartime.

ACKNOWLEDGMENTS

I gratefully acknowledge the support of the Corporation of Yaddo, the William T. Flanagan Memorial Creative Persons Center, and the Blue Mountain Center. I also wish to thank the following people: my editor, Janet Silver, who had the faith in me to publish a collection of stories; my agents, Charlotte Sheedy and Neeti Madan, for their caring work and guidance; Martha Upton, for her tireless reading of each of these stories and insightful suggestions; Linsey Abrams, my teacher, mentor, and friend, who always stressed to me the importance of finding my own voice; my family and my friends, who have always been an enthusiastic audience; and Linwood J. Lewis, my passionate reader, listener, and love. I am greatly indebted to the novelist Doris Jean Austin, who, before her untimely death, gave so much to the life of my work. Nothing will ever match her wisdom about the art of writing and the art of living. This collection was written in her memory.